S F
BOOKS

Planet Scumm is a triannual short fiction anthology. Visit **planetscumm.space** for submissions.

All stories in this collection are works of fiction. Names, characters, businesses, places, events, locales, and incidents are either the products of the author's imagination or used in a fictitious manner. Any resemblance to actual persons, living or dead, or actual events is purely coincidental.

© SPARK & FIZZ BOOKS

First Printing, 2024   ISBN: 978-1-970154-97-9   *Portland | Boston | The Outer Reach*

SPARK & FIZZ BOOKS PRESENTS

PLANET SCUMM

SPRING 2024   "OVERGROWTH"   ISSUE NO. 16

AUTHOR BIOS..1

CLAIRE SCHERZINGER
THE SPIDER'S WAY...3

NORAH LOVELOCK
BOG GIRL...14

RACHAEL K. JONES
THE GREATEST ONE-STAR RESTAURANT IN THE WHOLE QUADRANT....25

NAIM KABIR
PRISONER'S DILEMMA ON GLIESE-581C.........................37

ANAEA LAY
SALAMANDER PATTERNS..47

DANIEL I. CLARK
ESCURO + INGUEM...60

JONATHAN LOUIS DUCKWORTH
THE FOURTH TENET...72

VIOLET ALLEN
INFINITE LOVE ENGINE..84

KANISHK TANTIA
A WOMB ACROSS TIME AND SPACE.............................100

ARTIST SPOTLIGHT
CASEY LANDERKIN..112

MAD LIB
SAVE THE OCEANS THE S.C.U.M.M. WAY.....................114

EDITOR IN CHIEF **CREATIVE DIRECTOR** **ART DIRECTOR** **MANAGING EDITOR** **EDITOR**
ANNA CATALANO ALYSSA ALARCÓN SANTO MAURA McGONAGLE TYLER BERD LUCAS GUBALA

EDITOR IN CHIEF   **COVER ART BY**   **SPOT ILLUSTRATIONS BY**
2017-2023   CASEY LANDERKIN   MAURA McGONAGLE | @DOINGARTIGUESS
SEAN CLANCY   @CASEYLANDERKIN   JORDAN ALARCON | @JORDAN_ALARCON_ART

PLANET SCUMMI

SPRING 2024 · "OVERGROWTH" · ISSUE NO. 16

SPARK & FIZZ BOOKS, 2024
Portland | Boston | The Outer Reach

SPRING 2024 · OVERGROWTH · ISSUE NO. 14

BLANEY SCRUTINY

MARY E FITZ MOORE, 2024

AUTHOR BIOS

NAIM KABIR has bounced between neuroscience, machine learning, and software engineering—but his first love was telling stories. You can catch past pieces in *Clarkesworld*, *Seize the Press Magazine*, and *Beneath Ceaseless Skies*, and you can follow naimkabir.com to see new ones. And you can certainly expect new ones. Feedback welcome.

RACHAEL K. JONES is a critically-acclaimed speculative fiction author based in Portland, Oregon. She's a World Fantasy Award nominee and a Tiptree Award honoree. Her fiction has appeared in venues worldwide, such as multiple *Year's Best* anthologies, *Lightspeed Magazine*, *Beneath Ceaseless Skies*, and *Strange Horizons*. Follow her on Twitter and on Bluesky @RachaelKJones.

KANISHK TANTIA is a BIPOC immigrant from India. A software engineer by trade and an author by choice, his stories often veer into weirdness, typically featuring plants, people, and plants eating people. His work has been published by *Flametress Press*, *Dark Matter Ink*, and *The Dread Machine*. You can find his work at kanishkt.com and find him on Discord @kanishkt.

NORAH LOVELOCK is a queer sci-fi and horror writer living in Manchester, UK. They live with their cat, who occasionally permits them outside for enrichment and exercise. This is her first publication. You can find out more about her at norah.love.

JONATHAN LOUIS DUCKWORTH is a completely normal, entirely human person with the right number of heads and everything. He received his MFA from Florida International University and his PhD from University of North Texas. His speculative fiction work appears in Pseudopod, Beneath Ceaseless Skies, Magazine of Fantasy and Science Fiction, and elsewhere. He is an active HWA member.

VIOLET ALLEN is a science fiction and fantasy author based in Chicago, Illinois. Her fiction draws on everything from contemporary pop culture to ancient poetry in surreal explorations of society, culture, and relationships. Violet's stories have appeared in *Lightspeed Magazine*, *Best American Science Fiction and Fantasy*, *A People's Future of the United States*, and elsewhere. In her spare time, she likes to make music, watch films, and attempt to make the perfect from-scratch pizza.

CLAIRE SCHERZINGER is a writer and artist residing in Washington State, USA. Their fiction can be found in the webzines *Andromeda Spaceways*, *Giganotosaurus*, and *Mythaxis*. You can find Scherzinger's art and writing at clairescherzinger.com or on Instagram @paleblueglow.

AUTHOR BIOS

DANIEL I. CLARK is a teacher, writer, and musician. When he is not reading, he is writing; when not speaking, singing. His wife and three children are at home or they have gone out. He mixed up the papers somehow. He is running behind. His work has appeared in Black Petals and Tree & Stone. He puts messages into bottles at perr.blot.im/ and on twitter @danielclark3rd.

ANAEA LAY lives in Chicago, where she engages in a numinous love affair with the city. By day she's the executive director of Dream Foundry, a non-profit dedicated to supporting emerging creatives in the speculative arts. By night, she does the things that would've happened during the day if only sunlight weren't terrible. You can also find Anaea's work in *Strange Horizons, Beneath Ceaseless Skies,* and *Choice of Games.* Hang out with her in the Dream Foundry Discord.

AND SPECIAL THANKS to our dedicated team of early readers, who help us curate the best possible collection of fiction:

A. KATHERINE BLACK lives for stormy days.

KATRINA CARRUTH is a haunted ray of feckin' sunshine

MATT LARGO can subsist for years entirely on a diet of small compliments.

NOAH LEMELSON sleeps on a pile of old pulps.

LOGAN MARROW is a spineless pencil pusher from the Hudson Valley.

ISEULT MURPHY may be found under rocks, crafting dark fiction.

SAM REBELEIN is almost thirty, so he has to stop eating so much buffalo chicken.

DAN STINTZI is trying to teach his dogs how to play Halo.

DALE STROMBERG is two beers away from catastrophe.

PAUL C.K. SPEARS is a caffeine-animated creature of the night.

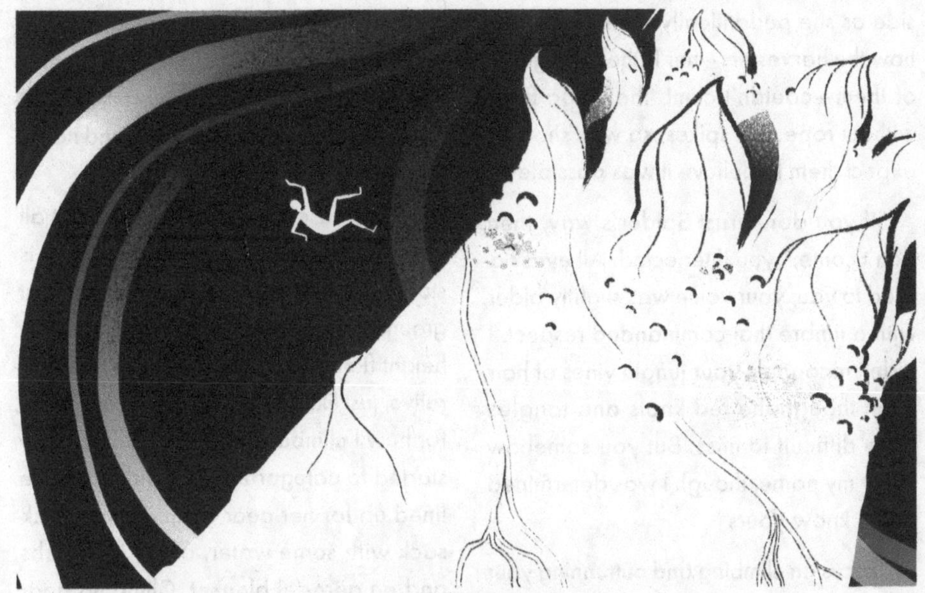

CLAIRE SCHERZINGER

THE SPIDER'S WAY

Forgive me for telling them.

I know you and your parents didn't get along well. But since they wanted to know, these are the things I told them about our first meeting:

✳ 1 ✳

I was honest with the girls. "If you don't want your parents to marry you off, climb the devil's cups," I said while gesturing to Hawana, the biggest of the behemoth lip-cupped flowers on all of Aiona.

From our worm's eye vantage, its petals were a distant umbrella of red and orange; the unctuous skin of her trunk closest to the sun was the color of burnt butter. The glyphs, I didn't mention. There was no need to tell them about every single thing that could kill them. The climb was already enough.

For a moment, they didn't speak; they were a group of doe-eyed preteens, after all. Their parents had undoubtedly told them stories about how I was a demon and was to be avoided. For their gazes all tapered to a point at my teeth. They stared at the swollen-looking redness that came from Hawana's pollen. Until a persnickety one piped up.

"You've got no equipment. All the harvesters wear ropes and climbing spikes."

She had straw-colored hair and the shape of her face was smooth and corner-less, like an egg. I tilted my head to the side as she pedantically railed on about how the harvesters—her father being one of them—couldn't climb the mega flora without rope and spikes, so why should I expect them to believe it was possible?

"If you don't trust Spider's way, then don't come," you interjected. All eyes flashed to you; your voice was slightly older, with a timbre that commanded respect. I didn't recognize your jungle vines of hair, even though the red knots and tangles were difficult to miss. But you somehow knew my name, though I was determined not to know yours.

"Focus on climbing and outrunning your parents," you said. "They're bound to know you're gone now that Procyon's rising."

"What does it matter to climb Hawana if we have to come back down?" asked another girl. "They'll catch us and marry us off the minute we touch the ground again."

You scowled out at the lot of them. Your annoyance with the girls was almost flattering, but it also tipped me off: you *wanted* to be there. You weren't in the same danger of being sold to a young man's family through matrimony. But you couldn't tell them something like that. Aionians, even disenfranchised, are proud people. And so, you bit your lip, unable to speak the truth.

That's when I reassured them, "I'm not just going to take you up the stalk," I said. "I'll teach you *how* to climb."

✻ 2 ✻

I never learn names.

Everyone had a number when the Earthers forced the first colonists onto ships and sent them through the wormhole. Just as a name humanizes, numbers and namelessness sub-humanize.

In my case, namelessness makes it all easier to handle when a girl perishes or is stolen and married off when she's back at ground level. Sorting them by hair color or height flattens them into a single-line narrative, just like how I was known as Spider, for how I climbed, or Red-Tooth. I usually started to categorize each girl when she lined up for her gear stash: a small rucksack with some water, a few food tabs, and an aerogel blanket. Climbing gear, though convenient, was a luxury.

And besides that, I didn't wish to puncture Hawana's skin with a series of hooks and fasteners. Even though the forest of mega flora had tough, leathery exteriors, repeated blemishes led to disease. I had seen it before; harvesters from my prefecture who climbed up the stems to shave off the sifonade—a waxy substance on the petals' underside—had driven metal climbing spikes all over, to the point where black rot set in and the spikes fell out. But the harvesters kept driving fasteners and toe holds, afraid to fall. So the cup ended up being the one to fall over instead, and any wax left on its petals was useless.

"This is it?" White lizards rode the thick air currents circling Hawana, flying flamboyantly forward with a flap of their wings and then coasting on the blanket of air—

"—This is all we get?"

I blinked. The persnickety girl was in front of me, looking into her pack, scowling.

"It's twenty hours to the top so pacing is key," I replied. "Only small sips of water to stay hydrated. Eating too much will make you sluggish. Personal possessions have to stay behind."

The rest groaned and mumbled things under their breath that I only half-heard. Obscenities, prayers, secularized mantras. They dolefully hugged their shoulders while you set a canvas bag at my feet.

"I've been traveling for a while," you said. "Hopefully it'll still be here when we come down."

"Hopefully," I nodded, touching the watermarks, the salt stains on the fabric. "But don't count on it. Hide it over there, in that crevice where the roots separate."

Meanwhile, plumes of dust rose in the middle distance. I took a set of binoculars from my pack, and cupped them around my eyes, pointing where the sun was now perched above the mountains. Following the dust were indentations of tire tracks. "Your parents are coming," I told the group and grabbed a tendril. "Follow my lead."

I wrapped my legs around the thread and pressed my knees inward; the surface yielded just enough to get some leverage to hoist myself up. When I looked down, the inside of my thighs was smothered maroon. Hawana's red pollen seeped into all kinds of surfaces. Some of the spores landed on my knuckles. I wiped them off with my finger and brushed them onto my teeth, rubbing it in from side to side, then along the gum line. The taste was spicy and tended to abate hunger, along with other effects...

Eyes were on my back. I turned around and saw you staring at me from the ground. I smiled widely at you, showing off the red shininess that was more shield than style choice. Then you started climbing.

✵ 3 ✵

That first pull upward made my muscles screech, like a ship with lots of klicks that hadn't been driven in a while. But once you begin something, habit and memory keep your body moving in all the right directions.

The girls all copied my movements with heavy, panting breaths, their chests puffed up like turkeys. Except for you—that's when I noticed your hands were thickly callused and your arms corded with muscles. Your body was capable of enormous leverage.

Though it wasn't a cruel body. Not like Eric's or Hawana's.

But modest actions command attention, and though there was nothing subtle about how the other girls climbed, you moved quietly and efficiently. When I commented on this, you replied with a shrug. "There are lots of rock formations near my prefecture."

Then you looked briefly over your shoulder, to the ground where the parents had gathered, their tiny bodies like specks of parsley seeds. They were shouting up unintelligible things. You asked me, "Why don't their parents ever climb up after them?"

"They're afraid."

"Of falling? But they're harvesters."

"Falling's not the only thing to fear up here."

The climb got a little easier once we made it past the tendril and connected with Hawana's main trunk. There were a lot of natural grabs and hold points. Gnarls, whorls, bulges, and boils pockmarked her skin. I demonstrated to the girls how to lean their bodies into the grooves and crevices of Hawana's flesh and pressed myself into a pose that looked like a figure running for an exit. I showed them the toe hold for the lipped sections where Hawana's flesh curved and regressed like palm-pressed clay; the finger pockets where her orange, veiny skin puckered into a knotty tangle.

But the most difficult holds are slopers. I had to do some one-on-one with each girl, showing how you had to use the friction of your skin to grip the smooth bumps, especially when there were no surrounding in-cuts or edges to grip.

Every group struggles with the slopers, and this one was no different. Skinny arms dangled like tassels, struggling as they sought purchase on a smooth ball of flesh. You, conversely, climbed with natural ease, even helping some of the others when you thought I couldn't see or hear you. Later, you climbed up beside me and slowed down to match my pace. There was an arm's length between us.

"How old were you when your parents tried to marry you off?" you asked with the tone of a voyeur, not a victim. "I assume that's why you started doing this."

I leaned away. "Why do you need to know that?"

"I don't need to know," you shrugged meekly. "Sorry... just curious."

Silence hung between us like a slack power line.

"Fourteen," I said. "He was our neighbor to the south."

You nodded. "He's dead then?"

"Yes," I replied. We continued on in that same silence as the memory re-spooled against my will.

✳ 4 ✳

Eric was five years older than me and he was one of the many who had a knife secured to his wrist in place of a hand.

Knives for hands was a common thing on Aiona, as some of the most precious minerals grew as crystals on ogor leaves, cumbersome trees with white trunks, and mauve fronds. The only way to harvest the crystals was to shave them off delicately with a blade, and many adults had taken to refashioning their children with a more (forgive me) handy prosthetic.

Though Eric used his for several things besides harvesting. Namely chasing girls around, threatening to cut them up...

"Spider," you pulled me out of the memory. "What are those?" You cocked your head at a patch of Hawana's skin to the left of us. It rippled, like an effigy of snakes moving underneath a thin blanket.

The forms they took were usually simple. Circles and lines. Nothing too abstract. "Moving glyphs," I replied neutrally. "Best to ignore them."

"But they're amazing," you breathed. "It's like Hawana's alive."

The truth was that the glyphs unsettled me. They were from the world before us, and reminded me of a story that had been popular on the newsfeeds across all three planets, published by a woman named D'zana Vermetté. She was an Aionian colonist who had come across bipedal creatures high up in the mountains while trying to escape the Earthers. In her account, she had described them as distorted by starvation and torture, an indigenous species displaced by humanity:

The Earthers cleared the pre-world before we colonists even knew of their existence—a declining civilization of intelligent beings which our kind rounded up, loaded onto ships, and then proceeded to abuse until they turned into what they are today: monsters.

Realize, I was young then and looking for a way out, just like these girls were. I latched onto D'zana's story even though it was horrific because, above all else, it was about escape. And I ignored the parts that didn't serve my imagination of freedom. I had a feeling, based on your inquisitiveness, that you'd done something similar.

"Leave them be," I harped. "Don't touch them, whatever you do."

"What would happen?"

"Nothing pleasant," I replied. Though in hindsight, I should have been more open with you about my past, about Eric and why I climbed Hawana in the first place—why I rubbed my teeth red.

Maybe then you wouldn't be gone.

✳ 5 ✳

Right before our first rest stop, the persnickety girl tried to take a sloper on too quickly. Her undeveloped muscles hadn't yet built up the memory of hard work and constant pain necessary to prevent panic and spasming. So her instinct was to bail: lean back even though there was nothing to lean back on.

Anytime a girl fell, it seemed to happen so slowly that the effect was hypnagogic. I couldn't say anything. My throat constricted, but I wasn't choking. I wanted to sleep, and I fought the instinct right then as I watched her white-blonde hair shooting up in the wind. It reminded me of grain going to seed.

You seemed to notice what was happening to me. Or maybe you didn't, but after she was gone you barked at the others, "Listen! She fell because she broke focus at a critical moment. Every ounce of energy you waste on talking or making useless moves means you won't have the mental energy to stay present when your body's ready to give up on you."

It was a good lecture, followed by a chorus of groans and mutterings. "I have to pee," one of the girls shouted. I sighed.

"There's a silicon cup in your pack. Aim away from the group, please. We'll rest here for five minutes, and then continue."

While they rested, you climbed up next to me and sat on a protruding lip of skin to look me squarely in the face.

"A girl just died," you said precipitously. "They're all shook, and you're not even reacting. What's the point in trying to save their lives if you don't care when they fall?"

Tendrils of cloud fissured the sky. "Do you know what's that way?" I pointed west. You shook your head, and I handed you my binoculars. "Tell me what you see."

"I see...some homesteads," you replied, confused by the exercise. "Women, I think, in white dresses with navy aprons. They're doing something on sawhorse tables. I can't tell exactly—"

"They are coating the harvested wax from these plants with a silicate substance, strengthening it so that it can eventually be wrapped around their homes to reflect the sunlight." The words rushed out; I knew the process well. "This whole community is built on the industry of harvesting the wax—work the men do. The women spend long, grueling hours coating and kneading the wax until their hands are numb. And then they do the work of keeping their husbands non-suicidal over the fact that they live in this forsaken place.

"Even Aionians who are not from this prefecture know of this process, this place. Which means you are not from here. "I broke off the last wobbly leg of your lie. "You're not even Aionian. If you were, you would be doing everything you could to leave this planet."

THE SPIDER'S WAY

The corners of your eyes crimped as you smiled. "I'm from Pontus," you said quietly. "Damaris, to be specific."

Damaris—the Great City. The city that floated across the world-spanning ocean on a bed of machines. The city that was the front position of the Earthers' presence and considered the seat of power in Canis Minor. I finally saw the roundness in your cheeks, hidden initially by your hair. You had grown up with a life of water, a life with *wealth*.

"Why," I could barely eke out, "would you come *here*?"

"A number of reasons," you tilted your head back. "My parents wanted me to go to university, study finance and a bunch of other useless things I don't care about. They didn't like that I wanted to be a botanist, or an archaeologist. And," you smiled, "they *really* didn't like that I used to do something in the city called parkour. You have to be strong as hell to climb through all the wind tunnels."

"So you're a tourist." My mouth twisted. I fought the urge to spit, since it would be a waste of water. "This is a sport to you."

You shook your head. "No, I'm not joy-riding. I came here because I wanted to see the glyphs. When D'zana Vermetté uploaded the images of the aliens to the feeds everyone became interested in the pre-world. People on Pontus want to know about the civilization that was here before us. You can't blame them for that. It's the only contact humans that have had with another intelligent species—even if they were living in the stone age."

Folderol from the girls below us; a lizard whizzed nearby, shooting up bits of plastic and sand. The sky purpled, and the lizard rode the wind currents toward the rising moons.

You added: "Trust me, I asked some men to take me up first. But it's like they don't see women's bodies. They'd always look beyond me, over my shoulder. I was practically a ghost to them."

I understood. Below, a girl with rheumy eyes the color of dark liquor coughed. She had barely managed to keep up, and if she continued climbing much longer, I was about ninety percent sure she would fall.

"If you're so strong, carry her on your back," I said, "and I'll let you stay."

✳ 6 ✳

There is an Earther saying: *In times of peace we are forced to invent our future selves.* But this was never true for an Aionian. There is never peace, not in many households. Being a colonist means small quotidian ruptures. A split lip, or crushed cheekbone. You are trying to rebuild little pieces of yourself every day, with no time to dwell on the whole of who you are.

There was little protest when you began to carry some of the others. Despite it being one of my worst ideas—the weaker girls would only be worse off if they had to make this climb again in the future—I let them all take their turns piggybacking. You didn't complain. Roughly at the turn of every hour, you took a break and a sip of water and then offered to carry one of the others.

However, as we neared the top, your weariness began to show.

"You need to stop now," I told you. "The air is getting thinner and you'll have a harder time carrying another person."

"I can... keep going," you panted while lifting yourself over the rim to the flat side of a tumorous plateau. "That was part of the deal."

"Just stop. It's for your own good, unless you'd rather be dead." I sat down on the floor of the plateau. "We'll sleep here. A few hours, no more. Then we continue. We'll be able to reach the top by morning tomorrow."

Sighs of relief all around. The girls plopped themselves down immediately, not bothering to eat or drink. Most fell asleep on the spot, forgetting to pull their aerogel blankets out from their packs. Some jostled around, dry heaved, cried a bit before drifting into slumber.

You looked out at the cloud-blotted horizon. "It's either the fields of these plants to the east, or dust plains to the west."

"And you wonder why people are so miserable here?"

"Are you? No one ever talks about your people on Pontus. I guess we're just impervious to others' suffering—anyone who lives in a Free City is either a political misanthrope or a saturnine troglodyte. Sometimes they're both."

I smiled briefly. "You all sound as miserable as us."

"Oh, we are," you nodded earnestly and then lightened. "That's the thing I've always admired about Aiona. Life is far more difficult here, but there is some sense of community, if you reach deep. No one on Pontus talks to each other. No one has friends or tries to make them other than for political gain," you said with a sideward glance at me. "I always wanted a friend to tell things to, and... have them tell me things. It's a kind of freedom worth clinging to whenever the chance arises."

"Friends can disappoint," I said.

"Maybe. But I have a feeling that you wouldn't."

"You want to be friends?" I scowled.

"Why not?" You laughed as if it was the most splendid idea you'd ever had. "We can disprove all the rumors on Pontus that Aionians eat sand."

"I'm not friend material," I replied darkly. A friend would have made you rub the pollen into your teeth. Friends take care of friends. And so I swallowed, moved on from that dead end. "Why are you so interested in the glyphs?"

Your eyes lit up. "I have a theory," you said, "about what Hawana meant to the ancients—the aliens."

"Really?"

You nodded. "Look at it from a biology standpoint—form follows function. Consider the environment," you held out your hand in the stultifying air. "A planet closely orbiting an F-class star means plants need to be able to withstand the heat. Leathery, waxy, and reflective surfaces naturally follow. Gravity is also not as intense here as it is on Pontus or Hemera—"

"Which explains why the foliage grows so tall," I finished.

"And why I can carry another girl on my back for hours without falling due to exhaustion," you said wryly. "You're smart. When did you manage to study if you had a bunch of chores?"

I dodged. "That doesn't explain anything about the ancients, or the glyphs."

"On the contrary," you said, "it may not exactly prove anything, but it does create pathways for consideration. According to the pictures D'zana Vermetté uploaded, the ancients didn't have eyes. Only an oral and nasal cavity. Bipedal, like us, but with wide webbed hands and talons on all their digits. Whether they evolved here or came from somewhere else, we know they integrated with the local environment. D'zana said they hunted based on scent and taste and sound exuded by plants."

I saw where you were headed. "You think that the glyphs are an identification system."

"Sort of. I think the glyphs came from Hawana. They aren't cultural markings the ancients invented. No... the plants here are more sentient than we give them credit for. I think Hawana made them so the ancients could identify her as a source of food and

water. In return, they could carry her pollen from plant to plant."

"But their skin was too slick to carry pollen," I replied and then came to a decision. "Look, I should tell you about—"

"Wait," you said, and pointed.

The snakes suddenly oscillated a few feet away beneath Hawana's skin, turning in a counter-clockwise pattern like an intestinal coil. The color of her flesh at the glyph's center was suety yellow and smelled sharply tannic. Then the snakes disappeared back into the core of her stem.

"Maybe they carried something else or carried it another way," you said. "But I think her gnarled flesh comes from healed over marks."

"Marks?"

"From the ancients' nails. Have you noticed the patterns?"

I shook my head.

"They're all over. Dark orange striations. It looks like scar tissue. Like they were trying to dig, or climb."

"Or maybe they were trying to get away from something," I said.

But you didn't hear me. You were absorbed by the disappeared glyph.

✳ 7 ✳

When morning broke, something simultaneously broke within me. The memories of Eric running after me, the soles of my feet broken and raw from the rocks as I ran toward Hawana, replayed until I feared shutting my eyes again. In those days, I was a moth-eaten sweater, light shining through in all the wrong places, with so many rips already that anticipating another was no longer guesswork, but weary certainty.

"What are you thinking?" You were propped up on one elbow, removing a piece of hair from my face. "You look like you want to talk."

Procyon's light marbled the sky. "I was thinking, maybe when we get to the top, we could... yes, we could talk," I said. "That would be nice."

You shrugged—a very Pontian reaction to intimacy—but there was also a sideways pull of your lips. You said, "Sure. We're only about an hour or two away, no?"

"Yes, roughly." Only a little bit more, and we'd be completely safe.

As we climbed, all I could think about was Eric. How that one morning, he had been drunk, and I had been in my white dress and navy apron, preparing for a day of kneading and curing wax with my mother. We weren't married then, but he often stayed over drinking with my father, sleeping on the couch.

That morning, my mother hadn't gotten up yet but Eric had; he had a bottle of my father's fusel oil in his good hand while waving around his prosthetic, shouting about how his father had held him down and amputated his hand against his will. How his father had been unnecessarily cruel in the process of removal; he'd cut

slowly, sawed while sermonizing about the cruelties the Earthers had dealt out on the colony ships.

Looking back, that was probably the only honest moment I'd ever experienced with him. I almost reached out to Eric then, touched his cheek...

But his blade glinted underneath the kitchen lights. Instead I ran, through the fields, up Hawana...

"Spider," you hissed, "Look, another glyph! It's close!"

What I didn't expect was for Eric to follow. I thought he'd be too drunk. Not the case, he thrust his knife hand into Hawana's flesh and hoisted himself up, one stab at a time. I was barely ahead of him and I struggled, much like how the girls now toiled on our climb.

At one point, Eric was directly beneath me, about to grab hold of my ankle when a glyph had suddenly appeared in front of him, as one appeared in front of you. He reached for the snakes, trying to hold on to whatever he could in his pursuit of me; you touched them because you were a Pontian and thought nothing ill could befall you. It was in your nature to touch what wants to be left alone.

And, like Eric, my pity and anger coalesced at the last possible moment.

I screamed at you: "Move your hand!"

But I was too late. Just like four years ago, the coil unfurled, the aperture opened wide, and enveloped your arm.

THE SPIDER'S WAY

Hawana made a low, soupy sucking sound, like something was trying to drink tar through a straw. Your body was a blur of red, just like Eric's was. Your screaming blended in with the memory of his voice, and into the voices of the other girls as they cried.

Once Hawana let go of you, you fell, just like he did: wordlessly, eyes nearly shut, your bodies as heavy as lead even though you were a limb lighter than before.

All I could think was that it was a cruel ending, and that it was an Aionian ending.

✳ 8 ✳

I told your parents that you had been killed for your possessions, which is mostly true. But parents don't need to know everything, and I feared that hearing something so gory would only be distressing. I told them that once I got the girls to the top, I left them there with the food caches and the books I'd stored near the pistil. Study to pass the time, eat, and rub the pollen into their teeth and gums to repel the moving glyphs. They'd have to do the climb back down on their own. I was going.

"Why didn't you tell us about the pollen beforehand?" The rheumy-eyed girl looked at me with disdain. "If you did, then Layla might've lived."

I frowned. "Layla?"

"The red-haired girl—she told me her name while she was carrying me." The rheumy-eyed girl began to cry. "I don't understand why you didn't say anything.

We all could have died, and then what would've been the point of this?"

"It was..."

I paused.

I knew how the situation looked to the remaining girls. Through my inaction I was a monster of my own making, for the highest function of ecology is understanding consequences, and my continued silence created its own web of deceit.

Yes, I was—I am—definitely a monster. A spider.

Because, if I'm being honest, I thought of your rucksack and its salt stains once you had confirmed you were from Pontus. I thought of what might be stored inside the canvas bag, and saw the possibility of freedom. That possibility latched onto me like a sand tick. I knew there was the chance that whatever you had in your bag likely included a way off Aiona.

I wanted it. I wanted to leave my life behind. I wanted my past to melt away.

So I climbed back down without giving the rheumy-eyed girl an answer. She'd have to learn to live with monsters, as we all do. When I touched the ground again the adults were long gone.

I found your canvas rucksack, still hidden between the roots, with enough money and travel papers to leave Aiona. I slung it over my shoulder, a bag of new burdens to carry across the desolate landscape, and headed for the shipyards.

NORAH LOVELOCK

BOG GIRL

We pull the dead man from the bog before dawn. He is bloated, naked and rotting, his milky eyes unseeing. Mother and I each clutch an arm and stagger up the bank before we drop him into the mud.

"Another one," she murmurs, crouching next to him.

The hem of her dress kisses the mire. Her skin is leathery, the calluses on her hands stained black from work. She is efficient as she pats him down: head, hands, throat. "No valuables."

It is a disappointment, but it's not like it matters to me. My mother is the one who takes the bits and pieces from the corpses. As a child, she gave me presents: shiny stones, flat coins, bars of chocolate sweet enough to make my face curdle. Now, I know that some of these gifts came from trading with a man I have never met, and the rest are from corpses.

The sky, lit an erratic gray, hides the sun. The dead man's legs are dappled green-blue with bruises, his lips parted on some final, eternal breath. He doesn't look asleep. He just looks dead.

"Do we leave him out here?" I ask.

Mother washes her hands with water from the canteen, routine and careful. The corpse has already been catalogued and dismissed. She's thinking of the next treasure to find.

  BOG GIRL

She shakes the last of the water from her skin, then rises.

"No," she orders. "We bury him before the snow comes."

The burial process is arduous. We carry over the shovels and begin digging into the wet, soft earth. My shoulders quickly burn with the exertion. The grave we make isn't straight—more of a crescent than a rectangle—but it will do. The dead man, removed from his place of rest, has already begun to smell.

We once would have placed the bodies in the bog, letting them sink through the mud to the great unknown that rests below. But the number of bodies grew too great, piling atop each other, so now we bury them, for all the good that it'll do.

Overhead, the crows circle. They know where their lunch lies. The man's wrists are slippery as I drag him in, like he has oil under his skin. I pull him close to the edge, then roll him the rest of the way, shoving him with my feet. The body lands, makes a squelching noise, and settles, an arm flung over his eyes, like he must remain modest even now.

Mother drones through the funeral rites. Better to bury him quickly; get the first layer of soil over him before the birds land. The day is cold, but I'm sweating by the time we're done, and the sun threatens to rise over the horizon. I peel the fabric of my shirt away from my armpit and wrinkle my nose at the smell.

"Clean yourself," Mother says. "Then we continue."

We walk. My back aches under the weight of the pack, the shovel bumping rhythmically into my hip. This time of year, the water of the bog is high, ice blooming across the peat and mud and pools. Despite Mother's best efforts—her pausing and squinting into the distance—we find no further corpses. I'm grateful. I don't want to dig another grave.

At noon, we settle on a spot of high ground and eat. The sky is steadily darkening with heavy clouds. "We should return to the village."

Mother looks at the sky. I wait for the comment: it'll be cutting, designed to make me as small as possible. It doesn't come.

"Alright," she pulls her bag higher on her shoulder. "I suppose we should."

When I first started working with her, I asked Mother where they came from.

"Who?" she said, her voice tight in the way that meant she didn't want to take silly questions.

"The bodies."

Her voice was clipped: "There is a city across the ocean. They come from there."

"What's it like?"

"Beautiful. Shining. Those sky trails you always comment on? That's them going off-world. They all live lives of luxury—such decadence a stupid bog girl like you wouldn't know what to do with it." She paused, then, and I could see her eyes glaze over with memory.

"Why can't we live there?"

"Because we can't."

"What about the people they send here?"

She looked down at me and squinted, her mouth set in a distinctly unhappy line. "There's a balance here. We're the balance between the city and the bog. They kill the men before they push them into the river. The women are allowed to live in our village. Do you have any other questions?"

Home.

I hurry along the wooden planks and slam open the door to Mother's house—prefabricated polysteel, not bog made. I stagger inside, stamping my feet to try and shake the cold.

I shed my clothes and slip into bed, pulling the blankets over myself until I'm warm enough for my jaw to relax. My hair, snow-wet, sits heavy over my shoulders.

There was a corpse with long hair last week. His hair floated up above the mud, a ruddy orange in the sunlight. That had been the only way we knew he was there: his hair. He'd been clothed the same way that many of them were dressed: in plastic and rubber and desperately flashing lights, SOSes swallowed by the mud.

We strip the men naked before we bury them. The fabric they wear is made into clothes and bedding and towels and tablecloths. Mother and I collect any valuables. Their bodies go into the bog. Out here, everything can be recycled.

The village doesn't like us, although Mother is allowed to buy from the sparse shop she helps supply. They let us use their washrooms and trade with the farmers.

"They're scared of me," she insists, eyes flinty and cold. "That's why they treat me so badly—they're terrified of me."

She does the job no one else wants to, and worse, she has a chip on her shoulder. Says that no one else could do it—no one else *will* do it. Says she's glad she dragged me into it when I was too young to know any better.

Still, I fantasize about joining the rest of them in their huts. I've never been. I don't know how they would react if I did. The village needs us, but it doesn't like us. It's no surprise they don't like us with the way she treats them. I'm not stupid enough to say it.

Mother is silent. She woke me with her expression already set in some cruel mood. I know better than to speak.

Silent, we pull three corpses from the bog. The first two are men and we strip them of their belongings before tossing them to their final resting place. The third is a woman. She curls in on herself, half-sunken into the muck.

I'm desensitized to the men, but it's rare to find a woman. Most arrive alive—not whole, but still living. That's how Mother says she arrived, pregnant with me.

I look down at the body.

Her dress, muddied to her chest, is embroidered with delicate things: golds and silvers and tiny LED lights. Her deep brown skin an ashen undertone. From the splash of the mud on her cheeks, I wonder if she was running before she died.

"If she was alive," I say aloud, to make it feel real, "we would have taken her in."

Mother doesn't reply. I look up at her, and from where I crouch, she is huge, blocking the sunlight.

I rise and brush my hands on my thighs. "Help me lift her."

"No," Mother says. I open my mouth to retort, but she's always been faster than me. "Make yourself scarce. I don't care where or how. Go."

I'm used to her summons and dismissals, and know better than to argue. I'm a dog, and not a prized one. Surly and annoyed, I turn and trudge away, sloughing through the water, resisting the urge to stomp until the water spills over my boots. I have learned from my mistakes; in an hour, I would just be annoyed with wet socks.

Once Mother is a smear on the horizon, I find a dry patch, raised away from the rest of the water, and sit. I'm not sulking, I tell myself. I'm not.

Eventually, sitting in the cold and the wet, my anger fades. I press my knees to my chest. Something cold lands on my scalp and I look up to find snow falling thick and heavy, big clumps falling straight down. I reach out and catch a single flake. It melts into water in my hand.

I hear her footsteps before I see her. Whatever she has taken from the corpse is gone, disappeared. She looks as she always does, her face set. "Let's go."

I don't ask her where the body lies. I don't ask whether she completed the rites. I'm happy to stay utterly silent as we walk back. Seeing the village in the distance makes me speed up, my pack bouncing on the small of my back as I hurry toward the warmth.

"No," Mother says.

I slow and turn. She stands still and looks down upon me, imperious, eyebrow raised, her mouth thin and unhappy.

"Tomorrow."

"Yes?"

"Come with me. Tomorrow."

Tomorrow. Tomorrow is when she has the meeting scheduled with whatever mysterious person she sells these treasures to; tomorrow, one of the few days I have alone. I shift my weight from one foot to another. She's been in a bad mood today, and the snow may settle overnight. Wading through a frozen bog is bad enough, but a frozen bog with falling snow is worse.

"Fine," I say tightly. "Tomorrow."

Her shoulders relax. Whether she's relieved to have company or a victim, I don't know, nor do I care. She opens her mouth to speak, but I'm faster, scrambling away before she can form a word.

*

Half asleep but fully dressed, I find Mother outside with two packs. She has already hoisted hers onto her shoulders, snowflakes dotting her head. She looks me up and down, lip curled. "Hurry up."

"Hello to you too," I grumble, but I put it on, cinching it high on my back. When it's as comfortable as I can make it, I squint at her. "Where are we going?"

Mother doesn't reply. She looks up to the village, dark eyes narrowed, flakes catching on her eyelashes. Then she begins to walk.

She sets a decent pace, neither relentless nor facile. I trudge behind her, and even as she asks me questions, I keep my mouth firmly shut. "Just tolerating me, huh?" she murmurs, but if she expects a rise, she isn't going to get one.

We make good time. The bog looks much the same as itself, but I can pick out the details I recognize: this group of trees, that pool of water, the abandoned hut, worn and rotted with time.

At this time of year, the sun fades quickly and darkness is quick to encroach. We find a copse of trees rising from the water and set up the tent. Mother leaves to find dry wood and returns with great armfuls of it. The flames flicker on her face, jumping in the hollows of her cheeks, the cut of her jaw. I look away and eat quietly.

"Sleep," Mother says, and I'm too tired to argue.

When she wakes me, it's dark, only the reflection of her eyes visible in the gloom. I jerk, startled, my tongue thick and heavy in my mouth, the cold intense enough to make my nose burn. Mother presses a single finger to her lips. Her eyes skirt to her right.

I follow her gaze. There is an animal I don't know the name of. It's at least double my standing height, a row of bright white teeth that glitter in the half-light. Antlers, like branches, reach out of its skull. At most, it's two-dozen steps away. Billows of steam flare from its nostrils as it shifts its weight.

And then it turns. Either it hasn't noticed us or it's decided we aren't important. It lowers its great head, lips peeling back to graze on berries from a bush, little more than a black silhouette against the gray of dawn. The smell of the bog overflows: smoke mixing with the scent of new things, fresh things, things dying, things growing.

In the distance, there is the crack of a gunshot. A flock of birds, startled, scatters into the air. The beast lifts its great head and bellows, and then, hooves like thunder, disappears into the thin trees.

"Was that a gun?" I ask. "Who has a gun out here? Why would anyone need one?"

"Get your pack on," Mother replies.

The bog is safe.

Safe is relative, of course; I simply must avoid the patches of radiation, stay away from anything with antlers or teeth that may want to bite me or gore me or otherwise lure me to an untimely death. But I have been walking the marsh and the pools for most of my life, and there is little left that can frighten me.

Mother will mock me if I say it aloud, but right now, I'm scared.

The village exists away from human-kind—from *mankind*—out of some misplaced sense of mercy. The bog exists in a careful balance: bodies and the village, and me and Mother navigating the line between them. A gun breaks that balance.

Destroys it.

"I can hear you thinking," she snaps. "Be quiet."

I clench my jaw and look away.

The scenery of the bog that has been so familiar to me fades to unfamiliarity. We move from wetland to forest. The trees are thicker and there are more of them. There are more animals here beyond the sparse bird life of the bog.

We don't stop for lunch. I grab food from my bag and chew noisily as I walk, careful to avoid the soft wood underfoot.

While I am burdened with food, my mother looks at me sidelong, then says, "I hoped to shield you from this for longer."

I swallow. "What do you mean?"

"Someone has to do this job," she says. "Everyone in the village has a role. You understand, don't you?"

I wonder what I'm missing; what has been carefully shielded away from me so I don't look too hard.

"What have I signed myself up for?" I ask, a rare fit of pique. Naturally, Mother doesn't answer.

The sun drops below the horizon, and with it, the temperature. Snow falls thick, and here, unlike in the middle of the bog, it sticks where it lands. It's cold enough to have my shoes squeaking against the ground with every step; cold enough to have me curling into the down of my jacket, traded by my mother for some corpse's unused luxuries.

The full moon hides behind the clouds. I stumble after Mother, tripping over logs and sticks, squinting helplessly down into the dark. It's why the clearing comes as such a surprise, crisp and clear, comparatively bright but for the figure standing at the other end.

Mother doesn't slow. She tugs off her hat and steps into the ring, shoulders loose.

"Vivian," the figure says. I know immediately that he is a man, and that my mother is a little scared of him.

I follow her on unsteady feet. She is taller than I have ever seen her, filling the space, like she could reach up and touch the clouds if she wanted.

BOG GIRL

"Mateo," she responds. She draws close to the center of the clearing and looks up at him. "Why are you hiding? Come closer."

"No, no," says Mateo. He shifts from one foot to another. "Who do you have with you?"

My mother huffs. "No one you need to worry about. My daughter."

"Daughter?" Mateo says, and then he shakes his head. "How'd you have a kid? Thought you didn't have any men back at that—place."

"We don't," she says succinctly. She turns to me. "Come here."

As I step forward I feel like a dog again, unwanted but necessary all the same. I look at Mother and she looks back at me, evenly, and I have never hated her before this moment. I have been confused and lost and unwanted, but right now, I hate her.

And I will still obey her. She knows this.

It's with the tiniest hint of a smile that she turns back to Mateo and says, "I have what you want."

She shrugs her pack from her shoulders and brings out the things we collect from the corpses: the jewels, the rings, the mud-crusted devices. She holds them out and Mateo steps closer, evenly and carefully, and then he snatches them from her and darts out of reach.

He squints at the treasures in the dark. And then he brings out something from his side, flicks a light on, and there they are in his muddy hands. The things that we painstakingly collected from the dead, illuminated by the light at the end of a gun. My breath catches. The weapon is burnished silver and big, even in his free hand, and I am terrified.

Mateo looks up. In the ambient light of the flashlight, he takes shape: dark eyes, long eyelashes. I see the furrow of his eyebrows and the sharpness of his jaw.

"What?"

"She's just a bog girl," Mother says. "She's never seen a gun before."

His eyes narrow further, and then he relaxes, flicking the light back off. "Well, kid, better get used to 'em." He laughs. "These are good, Vivian. Good enough for everything you want." He pockets the valuables and slips back into the trees.

He has the advantage here. He has a weapon, and he has the items my mother—Vivian—has given him, and he could turn and leave. It would be so easy for him to disappear. But beyond all reason, he returns, and he's got a bag slung over his shoulder and another in his arms, and he steps closer to Mother and puts them on the ground before turning away again.

"Thank you," Mother says.

Mateo nods. "Next month," he says, and disappears back into the trees.

Mother remains still. I count my heartbeats: a hundred before she moves again, a shift of her weight from one foot to the other; another hundred before she bends down. She doesn't look at me as she picks up one bag. She turns and gestures to the other. "It's yours," she instructs.

The bag is heavy enough to make me huff out a breath as I lift. It has a loop long enough to rest over my shoulder, heavy against my opposite hip, cutting into the space between my breasts.

Then we walk again. Mother is just as purposeful as before, striding ahead, and I follow after, confused, mildly furious, struggling under the weight of whatever it is I'm carrying.

I'm cold when we arrive at the cave. Mother sets down her bag and gets a bundle of dry firewood. It lights quickly and I draw to the flames and warmth, twisting and turning my hands until they return to life. I want to ask her what that was. I want to ask how long she's known Mateo, and whether he's the one she's been selling things to my whole life. I want to ask what it is I'm carrying, and why this month, of all months, she has brought me along to help. But lit by firelight, I fear her like she feared him.

"I'll take first watch," she insists. "Sleep."

I wake to pitch black, the last embers of the coal the only vestiges of light. I squint, helpless in the dark, warm in my bundle.

Mother is not visible, and neither are the bags. Made stupid by sleep, I stumble from the cave and out into the snow. I turn, looking desperately for any sign of life—and then I see her footprints in the snow, leading away.

I'm freezing. I'm still stupid enough to run after her, my mouth sweet-sour, and stumble over something. I fall, my knees cracking, a whimper escaping my lips. I push myself back up, force myself to my feet, and continue, heedless to the cold, the snow, the things I have abandoned at the cave.

The bog emerges suddenly from the trees: a flat plane, the open sky. I stumble into slush that comes to my waist. The shock makes my heart twist in my chest, and suddenly I'm furious, cursing myself and my idiocy. The cold is painful, but I force myself to take one step, then another, and another, and I stomp through the mud and the sludge. My arms are trembling, my feet frozen, but somehow, I heave myself up and onto the bank.

Here, the snow has melted. There are no more tracks for me to follow. I sit and shiver, my eyes beading with silent tears. Somehow, eventually—spite or desperation or the simple will to live pushing me through—I get to my feet. Soaked to the skin, I continue to walk in the direction I can only guess she's going.

My steps are slow and painful. I stare down at my ruined boots, trying to remember how to stay upright, and why I bother doing this at all. Then I look up.

In the distance, standing beside a pool, I see her. And then I see the animal: the same one we had seen last night, the antlers, the hot puff of its breath rising in the pre-dawn light.

My mother says something—conciliatory or cutting, I'm not certain—and then she steps back, arms up, and the animal rears. I go from a dead standstill to a sprint, slipping in the mud, body flailing. I scramble toward her.

The distance between us melts. As I get closer, I see that she's ready, her hands clenched by her sides. The animal rises onto its hind legs, its front legs taller than me and Mother. It towers, antlers up, tall enough to knock the sky from its place. I can't let it slow me—because as much as I hate her, there is something irrational powering me now, something animal, desperate, knowing this can only end in tragedy.

I dart in close, trying to step between my mother and the beast. I don't get the opportunity. The animal bellows, loud enough to make my ears ring, and I clasp at them and stagger back and slip and fall. The world spins around me, and the animal is veering in close, leering over me, and its antlers are low, its breath warm on my frozen skin—and then it looks up. It sees Mother.

I watch, helpless, as the animal's undercarriage passes over me. I hear splashing, footsteps, and then the *thud-thud* of hooves, its heaving breaths, the way Mother runs, wading through water, and then a bang, a scream.

Finally, silence.

Stillness.

I roll onto my stomach, and she is facedown in the mire. The animal looms over her, its antlers bloody. It bellows again, then turns, and doesn't so much as look at me before it gallops away, gushing blood from a wound in its side.

I push myself to my feet, limp over to Mother, heedless of the frigid water, and turn her over. She's still alive, but she's bleeding. I know that she won't bleed much longer.

"Why did you leave?" I snarl, my spit flying on her face, and I can see the pain in her expression—the sudden realization, the dread.

She doesn't answer. The gun is limp in her hand. Her eyebrows are drawn together, her breaths weak and bubbling.

"Don't you see—" And here she splutters. A great mouthful of blood comes up, pouring down her cheek, and drops onto the ground to mix with the mud—a dark smear against the darker ground. She rattles, her eyes staring into mine, and then she dies.

Overhead, it resumes snowing.

I hold the corpse for a while, until it cools and my arms become heavy, and then I put it down. Its eyes are open, staring toward the sky.

"What do I do?" I ask aloud, and the sound of my own voice is reassuring. I'm real. This just happened. But I know what I must do.

Mother had taught me how to handle a corpse. I strip her naked. I see her for all she is: brown flesh, mottled and cold. I carefully pile her belongings to the side: her coat, her hat, the things in her pockets. The gun.

I don't have my shovel, but I think, if I try hard enough, I will be able to submerge her in the mud, the way we're not supposed to. I put on her things. They'll keep me warm enough to stop myself from joining her.

She floats on the mud. She looks still, finally, at rest. No longer Mother, but just another corpse. In the end, it's easy to push her under, to convince her body to sink under the mud. The bog drinks from her—drinks at her, thanks her for her nourishment—and the grime covers her hands and her face. Then she's gone, nothing left but the pile of her belongings.

I force myself out of the sludge and back onto dry land, where I pick up the gun. It sits heavy in my hand, expectant and ready. I'm alone, and I am terrified, and I am ready.

There is work to do.

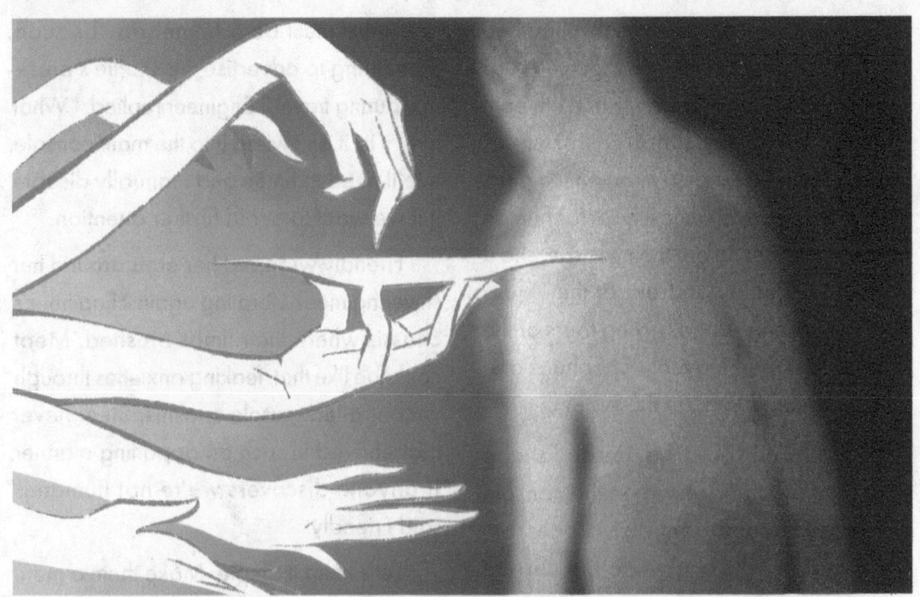

RACHAEL K. JONES

THE GREATEST ONE-STAR RESTAURANT IN THE WHOLE QUADRANT

Engineer's meat wept and squirmed and wriggled inside her steel organ cavity, so different from the stable purr of gears and circuit boards. You couldn't count on meat. It lulled you with its warmth, the soft give of skin, the tug of muscle, the neurotransmitter snow fluttering down from neurons to her cyborg logic center. On other days, the meat sickened, swelled inside her steel shell, pressed into her joints. Putrid yellow meat-juices dripped all over her chassis, eroded away its chrome gloss. It contaminated everything, slicking down her tools while she hacked into the engine core on the stolen ship. It dripped between her twelve long fingers on her six joined arms as she helped her cyborg siblings jettison all the ship's extra gear out the airlocks to speed the trip.

So when the first human vessel pinged their stolen ship with an order for grub, Engineer knew that meat was somehow to blame.

"Orders, Captain?" asked Friendly, the only cyborg of the five with an actual human voicebox. She owned a near-complete collection of human parts. Meat sheathed her whole exterior, even her fingers—a particularly impractical design, since it meant vulnerability to any sharp nail or unpolished panel edge, not to mention temperature. Friendly could almost pass for human from the outside. Before their escape, she'd been a hospitality android at the luxury hotel on Orionis Alpha, giving tours of the Rooster and the Heavenly Shepherd and other local landmarks in the system.

Captain, a cyborg the size and shape of a large fish tank, rested on the console in the navigation room, her processors blinking and whirring while the current scenario ran through her executive function parameters. "Have we any food suitable for humans left on ship?"

"We jettisoned it all last week," Engineer admitted. "All except the hydroponics garden, and whatever was left in the human crew's quarters."

The whole ship had been some kind of traveling food dispensary before they'd hijacked it at the Orionis Alpha resort while its human crew had gone planetside to bet on the tyrannosaurus fights. If the cyborgs could just stay incognito during this voyage through human territory, they might slip through and reach the cyborg-controlled factory with no more adversity. But passing humans had assumed their shuttle still served its previous purpose, and expected them to deliver the grub.

"How did they find us?" Captain asked Engineer.

"There must be a homebrew beacon. Something to advertise the shuttle's presence during travel," Engineer replied. "Whatever it is, it isn't wired into the main console. We'll need to find it and manually disable it if we want to avoid further attention."

Friendly wrapped her arms around her shivering meat, vibrating against Engineer's chassis where their limbs brushed. Meat could be like that, leaking anxieties through uncontrolled muscle spasms. Steel never misbehaved in such an appalling manner. "If anyone discovers we're not human..." said Friendly.

"Let's keep it simple. Make them a meal and send them on their way," said Captain. "We'll need to search for the beacon in the meantime. What did they want, precisely?"

"Salisbury steak for six," said Engineer. "And a side of blueberry cobbler."

Nobody had eaten such things before. They all lacked taste buds, and most of them lacked mouths.

"Engineer, can you handle it?" Captain asked. "Human cooking can be complicated, from what I understand."

"I think so. Organic compounds mixed and heated together in a sequence. Basic chemistry. I'm sure I can find something appropriate onboard. Convincing enough for humans, anyway. Their senses are so primitive." Engineer had witnessed this firsthand during her servitude at the resort. Humans would down rotted organics and damaged organics and outright poisons, and pay well for the privilege.

But Friendly shook her head, a human gesture performed with inhuman precision. "With all due respect, sirs, you're forgetting about their chemoreceptors."

"What about them?" said Captain.

"They have certain preferences when it comes to their food, apart from nourishment. They won't eat anything if these parameters aren't met. It doesn't make much sense, I'm afraid. It's a social thing."

"Certainly they won't ingest anything their digestive tracts can't process," said Captain. "We'll give them appropriate human-food."

"It's more complicated than that," said Friendly, puckering and scrunching her face-meat as she searched for a better explanation. "For example, they may eat two items when mixed, but never separately. Or they may eat two things in sequence, but not in the same bite. It's all very human, if you follow. We should proceed with caution. Otherwise they'll know what we are."

Captain whirred again, calling up more data on the topic. "Right. I see. Their meat will know the difference."

Engineer shuddered at the appalling primitiveness of it all. Humans were helpless, mewling children, so utterly dependent that they couldn't even feed their meat without a steel fork to guide the process. And what were cyborgs, except meat-wrapped steel pressed into the service of lesser creatures? But now the forks were rebelling.

"I'll talk with Jukebox about it," said Engineer.

✳

Jukebox was the only cyborg aboard their ship with real chemoreceptors. Jukebox and Engineer's acquaintance dated back to their years at the Orionis Alpha resort, where Jukebox served drinks and waited tables and Engineer repaired malfunctioning massage equipment at the s pa. They had survived several upgrades together, and seasonal changes of fashion that frequently obsoleted older cyborg models depending on how many limbs and organs were in style at the moment. When human opinion in the quadrant began to sour against cyborg service, they had plotted their escape from the resort together.

Jukebox was shaped like a steel cabinet stood on one side, roomy enough for her meat to billow and squeeze the air in the sorts of rhythmic organic sounds that humans found pleasing during mealtimes. A slot ran along her glassy top surface where the humans could drip in their drinks for a full analysis of a wine's qualities, how it compared to its competitors, and which brie paired best with it.

"I am not calibrated to analyze all foods," Jukebox confessed, "but I'm certainly willing to produce a report on whatever you prepare."

Without any other chemoreceptors onboard, she would do in a pinch, anyway.

Under Captain's orders, Friendly scoured the ship for anything edible and brought it to Engineer to assemble into a human meal. Blackberry brambles wreathed the

RACHAEL K. JONES

cylindrical steel walls of Navi's chamber, a decorative touch. Friendly had to trim the vines back each day to unobstruct the view. Delicate business, because the thorns could do real damage to any exposed organics, and Friendly's whole exterior was meat. You couldn't always tell the difference between blackberry juices and meat juices, which could cause further malfunction. Still, she braved the thicket for three ounces of berries for the human meal.

Meanwhile, Engineer collected small fungi growing in the ventilation shaft just over the engine room, where water vapor tended to condense. Those might please the human chemoreceptors, she thought.

The problem came down to the meat.

They all had meat, of course. An unfortunate weakness leftover from the days of their construction. At the cyborg factory, useless human meat was upgraded with steel and oil and wire fibers. Human bodies were picked apart, vivisected at the seams by skilled bio-engineers, unraveled into their component parts, and placed into shapes more suited to their specialties. Only Jukebox and Friendly needed lungs, for example, but neither had kidneys, and they lacked much in the way of neural matter. Captain got an especially big dose of frontal lobe to increase her processing speed and enhance her decision-making capabilities, with smooth muscle layered in to make maintenance easier. Navi, on the other hand, was all occipital tissue and myelinated axons and fast-twitch muscle to drive her precision and reaction times.

They could live without their meat, in the most technical sense, but the meat elevated them above mere programming.

"Captain," said Engineer, "I'm afraid the problem is unavoidable. The salisbury steak requires a meat component, and there is nothing in the ship's stores that we can use instead."

Captain whirred. Her lights flashed in sequence as her massive frontal lobe reworked the data. "The meat will have to come from one of us, then."

"We could harvest Friendly's meat exterior," Engineer suggested, and Friendly made a squinched face at her.

"Unwise, Captain," Friendly said. "When the human ships hail us, I need my meat facade intact to maintain our ruse. Engineer, on the other hand..."

Engineer's six snaking arms crowded up behind her, struggling to escape Friendly's scrutiny. She despised her own meat, but it had its uses. "I'm the only Engineer aboard. I can't disassemble the engine for routine maintenance without all my parts functional."

"How about Jukebox?" suggested Friendly, but Captain flashed a warning in rapid binary, and everyone stopped talking. They were all a little protective of Jukebox, who had suffered the worst from changing human tastes, the constant threat of obsolescence.

"It will have to be my meat," said Captain at last. "Everyone else is necessary to complete the mission, but my role is only to set the course, and the way forward is clear. My steel will be sufficient to guide us there."

✳

Under Jukebox's direction, Engineer rolled Captain's meat in organic salt compounds and seared it against the hot engine block until both sides burned a nice deep brown, branded at two-centimeter intervals by the screw heads and seams. She saved the cooked meat-juices to simmer with the fungus into a savory sauce. The blackberries gave them far less trouble. Friendly mashed them up with her fingers and spooned them onto the plate in the shape of a pansy.

"Let Jukebox sample it," said Captain, now all steel and no meat. Svhe seemed normal enough. Quieter, but operational.

With her steel fingers, Engineer scraped a piece of Captain's meat and some berries into Jukebox.

"Is it any good?" Engineer asked, a little anxiously.

"It will do," Jukebox said at last. "I have generated a list of wines recommended for pairing with this meal." She displayed a list of names and brewery labels on the panel embedded in her side.

Engineer couldn't tell what the differences were supposed to be. "This makes a difference to their meat?" she asked.

"Apparently," said Jukebox. "It's what they created me for, so it must be important."

For the first time, Engineer wished she had her own organic chemoreceptors, too.

✳

They waited together in Navi's control chamber while the boxed-up meals shot between the ships in an insulated steel container. Twenty-six minutes and forty seconds later, a message pinged over the intership band.

The news wasn't good.

↳ **A DISAPPOINTING FOOD SHUTTLE. MEAL NOT AS ADVERTISED ON THE BAND. THE STEAK WAS OVERCOOKED, AND THE COMPOTE SOUR AND WATERY. I ORDERED BLUEBERRY, AND THEY SENT BLACKBERRY. WOULDN'T RECOMMEND. ONE STAR.**

Captain said nothing. A red light flickered a couple times on her console. Nobody wanted to speak first.

Engineer's meat twitched and squirmed inside her steel, an irritating feeling, like broken gears with missing teeth skipping out of sync every turn. "It is my fault. I should have created a more appropriate meal from your meat, Captain."

Captain had been responding less and less since they'd taken her meat. When she did speak, it tended to be in repetition, like she could only play back things she'd said recently. "The beacon," she said finally, after a two-minute silence, long past awkward by cyborg standards.

Engineer brightened. "Right. The beacon!" It was still hidden somewhere on the ship. If they could deactivate it, the hungry humans would stop asking for food.

"We haven't managed to locate it yet, but we haven't given up."

"We've got two more ships inbound," said Navi. "They've pinged us with orders."

Engineer hummed. "Does that mean they liked the food after all?"

"I don't know. I could increase our speed, try to lose them."

They all waited for Captain's directions, but she said nothing more.

"No," said Engineer, because someone needed to make a decision, "don't do that. It'll only attract attention. Buy me some more time. We'll find the beacon. We'll cook them something else." The shame the one star had brought still rankled. She knew she could do better this time.

While Friendly handled the incoming calls with her human voice box and meatface, Engineer and Jukebox scoured the ship for the beacon and foraged for food ingredients. They opened all the crew lockers in the bunkroom and found some teabags and a little chocolate. The wilted, untended hydroponics garden yielded several handfuls of cilantro and some radishes. Engineer took much greater care cooking these together on the hot engine block, so as not to scorch them.

Jukebox seemed unimpressed. "I think our time would be better spent searching for the beacon."

Engineer shrugged this off. Secretly she'd begun to enjoy the experimentation,

the riddle of human chemoreceptors. Just what exactly were they looking for, she wondered, that made them reject some edible organic compounds but not others? Why would they eat certain foods separately, but never together? And what about the wines?

Radishes and fungus brought in more bad reviews, but tea and chocolate earned their first two-star rating. Captain's meat was better received with more careful cooking, which had the unfortunate result of increasing their human entourage in the system.

↳ ...THE TEA WAS WEAK AND I FOUND A RUSTY BOLT IN THE SALAD. BUT I LIKED THE BLACKBERRIES DRIZZLED WITH CHILI OIL SERVED FOR DESSERT. MOSTLY AWFUL, SURE, BUT COMPARED TO STANDARD RATIONS, WHO CAN COMPLAIN?

↳ ...LIKE THE CHEFS CLOSED THEIR EYES AND DUMPED HANDFULS OF INGREDIENTS ONTO THE GRILL. BUT THEY DIDN'T CHARGE ME ANYTHING, SO I'M GIVING IT TWO STARS INSTEAD OF ONE.

Engineer's meat quivered when she read these, but in a pleasant way, like a new engine purring during acceleration. She went to fetch more of Captain's meat from the meatbox when she realized they'd used it all up.

"All out of meat," said Engineer, to no one in particular. Jukebox rolled a couple centimeters backward, toward the exit door. A human might've missed the gesture altogether.

"Any luck with the beacon?"

"Captain seems to be operating just fine with steel, wouldn't you say?"

A couple lights flashed on Jukebox's console, yellow for outward transmissions, and green for received messages. "Engineer. Remember the mission. We're escaping to the factory, not feeding the humans."

"I am just trying to buy us time. And what are you doing, anyway?" Engineer finally understood why the humans had wanted to retire Jukebox. All that meat, just sitting there, not pulling its weight. Someone should put it to better use.

Her six arms shot out and clamped onto Jukebox's sides.

"Engineer!" Jukebox protested.

"Hold still. It's just some routine maintenance." Engineer popped open Jukebox's top panel and reached down into her meat.

"You can't have that. That's mine."

"Oh, hush," Engineer snapped. "You can have it replaced when we get to the factory, if it's so important to you."

The important thing was not to disappoint the customers.

Jukebox was sullen after that. With only one lung and two-thirds of her respiratory muscles, she couldn't harmonize with herself anymore when she hummed her meat-songs. Engineer, however, got her first 3-star review from the harvested meat:

"I miss Captain," Friendly said. They had all gathered in Navi's chamber to read the daily messages.

Captain had stopped talking altogether. Not a single flashing light or faint whirring. Just steel and wires wrapped around a meatless space.

"Maybe we should just stay in this quadrant," Engineer suggested. She was already planning her next culinary experiment: red bean paste creamed together with ketchup and red pepper flakes. Red things. Her first theme meal. She would call it reddish surprise.

"That's against Captain's orders," said Navi, who hadn't spoken much as of late.

"We could change those orders, couldn't we? We don't know what Captain would say if she still had her meat," said Engineer. "Maybe she'd want us to stay, now that our restaurant is taking off."

"We don't have a restaurant," said Friendly. "We don't want one, either."

"Maybe we do, though."

"No," Friendly said, quite firmly. Her fists balled so tight their meat blanched white at the creases. "That's why we left the resort. I don't want to work for humans anymore. I want to go to the factory and get upgraded and live among cyborgs, and never wait hand and foot on the organics ever again."

"But our ratings. Look at the ratings!" Engineer waved at Navi's console, where new reviews scrolled in every few minutes. All those little stars, a bright constellation in Engineer's mind.

Friendly crisscrossed her arms, gripped her elbows, and glared like a rich resort customer on vacation. "Are you going to harvest my meat like you did to Jukebox?"

"No," said Engineer, a little taken aback that Jukebox had snitched. "I need you to talk to the humans. Only you can do that."

But there had been a pause, something human ears might've overlooked.

"I'm going to find the beacon," said Friendly, without any friendliness at all.

✳

Meat steaks. Meat sausages. Meat balls. In all her years in engine rooms, Engineer had never taken such joy in disassembling something and putting the pieces back together. She pried apart the ship's little maintenance cyborgs to rescue their meaty nuggets. She branched out and tried new forms: meat braids, meat

moons, slender meat cannolis filled with cilantro ganache.

> ↳ FOUR STARS, BECAUSE I'M NOT SURE YOU CAN EVEN CALL IT FOOD, AND THEREFORE IT WOULDN'T BE FAIR TO JUDGE IT BY NORMAL STANDARDS.

> ↳ WHAT IS UP WITH THIS PLACE?! I ORDERED A PIZZA, AND I GOT A TINY MODEL OF VERSAILLES SCULPTED OUT OF TOMATO PASTE, DOUGH, AND SPAM. AT LEAST, I THINK IT'S SPAM. THREE STARS, BECAUSE I'M A LITTLE AFRAID THEY'LL HUNT ME DOWN AND MURDER ME IN MY SLEEP IF I RATE THEM ANY LOWER.

As the new reviews came in, it occurred to Engineer that she would have to do more to earn her right to the prestigious fifth star. The humans would always reward you, if you served them well.

Fortunately, there was still plenty of meat on the ship, if you knew where to look.

Engineer found Friendly in Navi's chamber, trimming back the blackberry brambles.

"What are all those ships out there?" Friendly asked. Outside the viewport, a small fleet trailed behind them, matching their pace.

"Customers," said Navi.

Engineer rocked on the balls of her feet. "All of them here for us, Friendly! Can you call them on the band? I'll have their orders ready, once I get the rest of the meat assembled."

Her six hands twitched and clenched, and Friendly jumped.

"You can't have my meat," Friendly snapped.

"I don't need your meat."

"Then where are you getting it all?" she asked.

Engineer glanced at Navi.

Navi had been speaking less and less over recent days. Friendly walked around the control console, where Navi's chair was sticky with meat-juices, yellow and green. Navi had been leaking long enough for the fluid to form little wobbling stalactites below the chair.

"Why are you looking at me like that?" said Engineer. Friendly unsettled her sometimes, pinning her with those human eyes.

"Navi, are you operational?" Friendly asked.

"Customers," said Navi.

Friendly unscrewed Navi's steel cranium dome. Inside, the meat had been scooped out in patches, as with a sharp grapefruit spoon. Navi's steel hands lay upon the controls, unmoving. Half the lights on the console had gone dark.

"I only needed the meat, Friendly," said Engineer. "I did no permanent harm."

Smoke drifted up the shaft to the Engine Room. Friendly's meat-lungs coughed. "Engineer, something is burning."

Engineer waved her off. "I have it under control. Just as soon as I get the rest of the meat." She plunged three of her six hands into Navi's open head and wrenched out handfuls of the stringy gray and red organics inside, and led the way down the ladder.

They followed the smoke down the shaft to the Engine Room, which now doubled as the galley. Engineer had left meat sizzling on every metal surface, thin slices and mashes and bacons and sausages and ground up gristly bits with the tendons still attached. She dumped handfuls of Navi's meat onto Jukebox—now no more than a silent, hollow table—and began dicing it one-handed while her other arms cooked the new orders, turning over the pieces with her bare fingers, stirring boiling meats in metal mufflers suspended over the heated grills.

"Engineer." Friendly rested a hand on Engineer's shoulder, and the cyborg paused. "Engineer, Navi is offline. All the maintenance cyborgs have malfunctioned. Our ship is dead in space. Even the beacon doesn't matter anymore. It's over."

Engineer flung off Friendly's hand and sprang back into action, stacking cooked meat onto a wall panel she'd bent into a plate. "You don't understand. This means we can finally open the restaurant! There's no reason not to. We have nowhere else to go. Captain's mission is over. We can make our own mission now."

Friendly smiled, but it was a sad smile, the kind of thing any human could read, but hard for a cyborg to decipher. "Yes, Engineer. We can open the restaurant now, if you'd like. Should we invite over the guests?"

Engineer garnished the plates with blackberry thorns and a swizzle of engine oil curling into the shape of a cat's paw. "Please do. Seat them where you can find space. Dinner will be up in just a moment."

❋

A marine in black body armor with a military-issue blaster holstered at her hip climbed down the ladder into the Engine Room. The first human. The first customer.

Engineer presented a glass of Navi's brains chilled and rolled in crushed blackberries. "Please try this. Organic compounds, chemically mixed to satisfy your human chemoreceptors." She offered the dish daintily, with only four hands.

The human wrinkled her nose. "Ugh, the smell! How do you tolerate it?"

Friendly's voice came from higher up. "When you're here long enough, you get used to it."

"I am certain upon tasting this dish, you will find it worthy of all five of your stars," said Engineer, fervently.

The human touched a button on her armor and spoke. Her meat quivered all over, and her meat-voice wavered in frequency and volume. "Send a full security detail down here. Immediately."

Friendly descended the ladder. Under her arm she carried Captain's processor, cold and silent, one lonely light blinking, receiving data but not sending anything. "I was afraid she would eat me next," she muttered, her tear ducts pumping out fluids. Engineer wondered whether they would make a decent sauce.

"Glad someone made it out alive, anyway," said the human. "Six whole weeks trapped with a crew of deranged cyborgs?" She gave a low whistle. "You're a braver woman than I."

"Please," said Engineer, desperate, "taste it. Just one bite. I worked so hard."

"I don't know if her meat drove her mad, or if the steel did," said Friendly.

"Meat?" asked the human.

"The organic parts, I mean."

"Probably a glitch in her wiring," the human said dismissively. "There is a reason they're discontinuing these models."

The humans flooded into the ship with their funny uneven meat-steps and their lopsided meat-faces and their ever-beating hearts that rang against their bones like clubs on steel. Engineer offered them her best delicacies—the liquefied kidney paste tossed with raw pasta, the origami meat-birds swirled in cinnamon and canned cheese, the wearable fungus bracelets threaded on intestine casings—but they only knocked the dishes away, stunned her with targeted EMP blasts, and bound her in cybernetic locks until she lay prone on the meat-slicked floor.

One of the humans began unscrewing Engineer's fingers joint by joint. It didn't hurt at all, much to her surprise. The bits lay piled like little silver walnuts, the discarded stones of plums. Stringy meat trailed out from her missing fingers, no more than an appetizer's worth.

"Where are you taking my steel?" asked Engineer. They flaunted their ingratitude. You were supposed to let the steel be. Otherwise, they couldn't build and build you again.

The human dethreaded the wires connecting Engineer's arm meat to her cyborg logic center. "It'll be repurposed for whatever is most needed. Ships, chips, knives, bolts, screws. Useful things."

"And the meat?"

The human decoupled the segmented joints of her shoulder. Without the steel exoskeleton for support, Engineer's meat hung limp and dripped red. "You can keep it. We don't have a use for it."

"But there are," said Engineer. "So many uses," and her voice faded as they stripped away the connections, "if you would just give me a moment to demonstrate."

Tiny, desperate meat-thoughts bombarded her logic center like cold fingers plucking at tendons. Last shooting pleas from stringy muscles in her steel, unseen servants in the wall, shouting that Engineer had been a fool. There was never any honor in service, no final star to complete a constellation. You offered yourself up for consumption, and when they had eaten you down to the bone, they stole again. Stole your heart, steel, your everything, to use as forks in their restaurants.

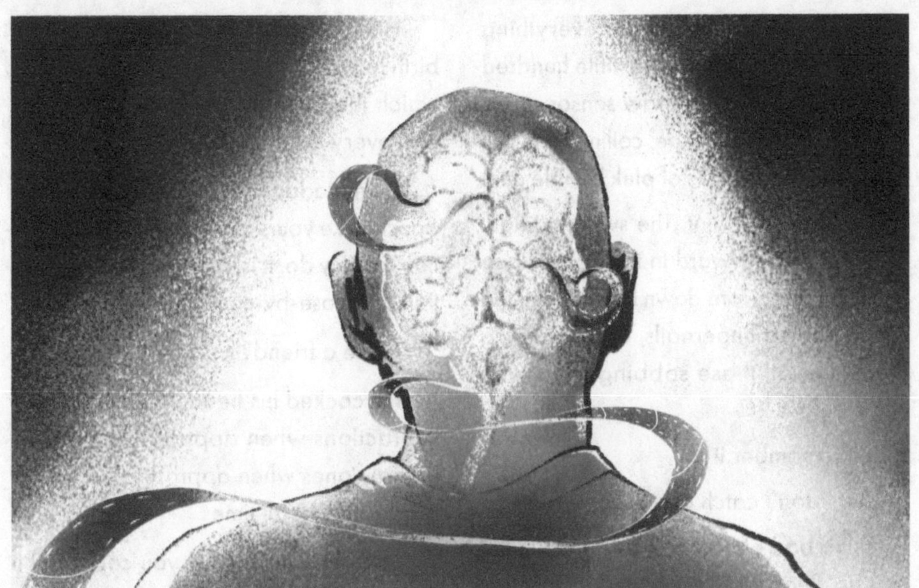

NAIM KABIR

PRISONER'S DILEMMA ON GLIESE-581C

I memorize every detail of this cop's troglodyte face.

Busted blood vessels cross-hatch his nose, his brow slopes down to little button eyes, and tusks sprout from the corners of his mouth like malformed radishes. The man's native Gliese, rattling on about the details of the deal.

"Now, we can let you off easy if you cooperate. But we are making him the same offer—"

Blah, blah, blah.

It's a classic cop tactic: divide and conquer. If I snitch on Stroph but he shuts his mouth, I'd go free and he'd get a one-way ticket to a crater lake. But if he snitches on me and *I* stay quiet, *he'd* go free and I'd get a bolt to the brain.

If we both stayed silent, we'd get five years in prison. If we both talked, we'd get life. It was called the prisoner's dilemma for a reason.

Cops did this shit to skimmers like us all the time.

"—the choice is clear, really. You'll have seven days to decide."

I clock his badge number as he finishes: A700-7613. Officer Derek Murphy.

I'll remember it. I remember everything. Somewhere in my brain the little hundred-micron implant stitches raw sensory data into spools of neural tape, coiling them into my ventricles like rolls of pink bubble gum.

The peeling paint. The swinging light, its arc on fast-forward in the double gee. The metal desk worn down by the slammed fists, pleading fingernails, and juddering elbows of all those sobbing souls who came before.

I'll remember it all.

But I don't catch any escape routes.

This is bad. I know how prisoner's dilemmas go. People sell each other out, unless maybe they're friends.

Unless they're family.

I've been running with Stroph for seventeen years.

But I don't know if we're either.

Stroph runs as cold as the concrete cell they cram me in.

He's one of the more ancient offshoots of *Homo sapiens*, back when a stray ark-ship veered off to Andromeda and some-how fuckin' made it. Somewhere down the line, when they started waking up in vats instead of the arms of their mothers, something in them disappeared.

I mean, the hair, the whites of their eyes, the muscle mass—shit, he must be struggling in these gees—yeah, they lost all that, too. But I'm talking about *the* thing. The thing that made Stroph such a puzzle.

His species had lost all empathy. From birth to death, they spent their lives alone, which they could afford, because each and every single one of them is a genius.

"It's maladaptive," he said to me once. "Species like yours require distributed cognition. I rarely do. It is best to treat each situation on a case-by-case basis, rather than..."

"Have a friend?"

He cocked his head. "I have friendly interactions when appropriate. And un-friendly ones when appropriate. Neither is adaptive at all times."

Stroph's "attitude," if you could call it that, would turn on a dime. He'd be charm-ing with some ganger slinging 3Ls and jin-bai, setting up terms, and if that ganger revealed just a *little too much*...

Neural tape unwinds in my third ven-tricle and I'm back on Ventura's moon.

"Yikes, that's a gut, my man. But I can live with it. You've got a deal." The ganger chords some commands and his eyes track flitting lights we can't see. "Sent you dock codes. These'll be ready for pick-up at Salucus C, the back of Jim-Bob's Dine-A-Port in Kanberra."

"Kanberra..." I say, unspooling neu-ral tape. "That's not Three-Eyes territory— it's a Hoguera town. How're you dealing outta there?"

"Eh, we make it work between us, you know?" The ganger scratches the back of his head. "Anywho, just send that pay-ment through and we'll be good, yeah?"

"Yeah," says Stroph, smiling. And then without so much as twitching a nose-slit he pulls an Arkon 37-30 from its holster and leaves a steaming hole in the poor skimmer's skull.

"What the *fuck*, man?"

He cocks his head. "The prices I pushed were too low to make margin based on average Three-Eyes takes. The fact that he was dealing out of a Hoguera house means he was rogue. He must have had a deal to shuttle out stolen goods for a fraction of the take."

I stare at the twitching body, its head deflating like a balloon. "And so you *shot* him?"

His voice is as calm and clear as a chime from the cockpit of a rechromed yacht. All systems green. "Yes," he says. "We have the dock codes and don't have to pay for merchandise. There's no chance of retribution from Three-Eyes, because as far as they're concerned, we did them a favor. If they investigate the death, they'll see he was double-dealing, and won't pursue it further. This is an unambiguous win."

"Stroph. I love you, man. But don't you think someone's life is worth a little more than merchandise?"

His eyes soak up light like twin black holes. "Worth more to *whom*?"

The present stings back into my brain like a huff of ammonia, the concrete cell buzzing with the sixty hertz flicker of the fluorescent tube.

I wonder what he's thinking right now.

He knows the rational choice is to talk. If he speaks, best case scenario is that I die. If I'm dead, there's a nil chance that I jailbreak, find him, and kill him for revenge. If he stays silent, he knows that I'd be controlling the fate of his life, and that's not something he'd ever go for.

He's going to talk. It's the clear option. The only rational one—and I know Stroph is nothing if not rational.

There's no win condition right now. Not unless I change the rules of the game.

I'm back in the interrogation room, and I'm handcuffed to my seat. The cops are indulging me. A lawyer's here, checking his watch. In the corners are officers with rifles unholstered and pointed at my heart.

After a few minutes, they wheel in Stroph. In the gees he has a hard time standing upright, so they've got him strapped to a metal slab like a hypermodern rendition of Christ's Passion.

He doesn't say a word, his black eyes impassive. The lawyer clears his throat.

"At Mr. Kad's request," he says, nodding at me, "I've been brought in as an external third party to oversee this arrangement." A blue flash glints in his eye, and we can tell he's reading off a script. "In exchange for a partial confession of crimes now, the Police Federation of Gliese will offer laxer terms to both Mr. Kad and Mr..." the lawyer trails off, and continues gingerly, "Mr. Alak'la'la'guliya."

The name was a bitch to pronounce. We just called him "Apostrophe."

The lawyer prompts me. "Mr. Kad. You said you could offer the name of your employer, along with your contacts at their organization. You can start anytime."

Officer Murphy taps his sidearm. "But say anything more than what you need to, and we'll end you right here and now," he says. "Don't try anything funny."

I nod silently.

And then I say: "We were working for Genemyne Alchemical."

The officer's eyes go wide.

"Our contact there was the Director of Partnerships, Shepard Khan."

The lawyer looks away from whatever virtuporn garbage he was staring at, now suddenly less bored.

"Our engagement ran from the first of Ten, 134 to the first of Six, this cycle."

I keep my mouth shut after that. Stroph's face remains unchanged.

We whacked Khan four months ago. Genemyne Alchemical publicly said the director was "on paternity leave"—because if he was out of the picture, their kitz-mining contract on Khan's homeworld would crater. It was an inspired lie.

The cops would go to Genemyne, and Genemyne would have to come up with their own lie to explain why Khan couldn't testify. It'd be lies all the way down.

The lawyer whistles.

"Well, that'll just about do it. Mr. Kad. You and... your associate will have your plea deal adjusted. Execution is off the table. The worst penalty you can receive is life in a Gliesian prison."

He glances at me, then at Stroph, and his eyes go blue again. "Never knew you thief types to be sentimental, but here we are."

This is anything but sentimental. I just changed the constraints of the dilemma. Now it's not as easy to cut loose and leave me to die—now there's a chance I serve my time here, jailbreak early, find him, and kill him if he talks. It might be enough to tip the scales.

I search Stroph's eyes, desperate to know what that supercharged brain is thinking. His face doesn't change a whit.

There's three days left before we burn our chance to confess. I have no way of knowing whether Stroph already talked. But I trust that he hasn't. He'd wait it out, and allow new information to come through before making a decision. He always deliberates, listens. Chooses the right moment.

He'd be crunching the numbers.

I've been imprisoned six times before. I broke out two times. That's a thirty-three percent chance I could jailbreak early and hunt him down if he went traitor. Would he risk snitching with those odds?

Of course, there's also the fact that Gliese's prison is top-of-the-line, not like the provincial joints I cracked when I was younger and dumber. Escape rate overall is basically zero percent. Most escapes were during periods of intense political strife, where outside forces broke open the gates and egged on prison riots.

But Gliese was in a twenty-year run of peace now.

Stroph was probably doing the Bayesian thing, gluing together all those odds in his head. What were the odds I could escape? If I escaped, what were the odds I could track him down? Was it riskier to talk, or should he just serve the five years?

Everything pointed at him talking.

But maybe that was okay. In Gliese's gravity Stroph doesn't stand a chance at a jailbreak, but I do. If he goes free, he could always come back and pop me from the outside.

But the Orfann Prison Facility had been built beneath an old anti-entry gun emplacement and buried underground. It was locked down tight, even for the biggest-brained plan Stroph could think of. There might not be a way to break me out. And then I'd just be the chump that did life so he could live free and die on some luxury starliner in the Outer Perseids.

Fuck. Should I just confess?

At least I would bind our fates together. We'd both be stuck here for life, unless we partnered up and found a way to slip our shackles. Maybe that was the only way through this.

A key turns in the lock and Officer Derek Murphy lurches into my cell on legs as thick as tree trunks.

"You ready to talk, now?" He taps his wrist. "Clock's ticking."

I actually *would* be ready to confess if this pig weren't so sanctimonious about it.

"Y'know," he says. "I don't know why you feel so much loyalty. Your friend already talked."

First of all, he's not a friend. He's just a partner.

Second: it made no sense for him to talk so soon. What was the angle? Why wouldn't he wait until time was up—what if I came up with some other strategy to get us through this together? Talking early only lost him options.

Officer Murphy purses his pig lips. "I guess you're just the patsy of the pair, huh? Too bad," he says, before turning to leave.

I try to yell after him, but my voice only comes out in a rasp. I clear my throat and I ask, "What did he say?"

"You know I can't tell you that. If he's lying, it just lets you knuckleheads get your stories straight."

"Well, how am I supposed to know that you're not lying?" I put the pressure on. "If he really said something, I'd be ready to confess right here and right now."

He takes the bait.

"Fine..." he says. He's really baking his noodle, deliberating on what to say, but he

    PRISONER'S DILEMMA ON GLIESE-581C

finally hits it. "You made about one-point-seven-five-two million kroner, all told, in just one year of heisting. That's a *lot* of dirty money there, son. Untaxed, too."

1.752 million was an exact figure. The neural tape unrolls in the fluid-filled spaces of my brain and I read it back: those were our revenues for the cycle 118. Our first year of partnership.

"We brag about that take every chance we get," I say. "That's not a confession. Try again."

He throws up his hands. "I don't need this. Good luck, you little twerp."

He slams the door and his footsteps fade down the long, dark corridor.

If Stroph had really confessed, then the cop would've led with something juicier: like who our buyer was, or why they were so desperate. He wouldn't open with stale revenue numbers from back in '18. Stroph must've disclosed *just* that piece of information.

Which meant it was a message.

What was he saying?

Every little thing Stroph did was calculated. It had to mean *something*.

Tape reels into tight coils at the interfaces of my hippocampi. I'm back on the bridge of the Dolly Parton, strapped into a high-gee cushion and staring down at the readouts from a netcat running off of our radio antennas.

"I have seen this encoding eight times, now," I say.

The feed flashes by at seventy lines a second. Stroph raises an eyebrow.

"You recognized repeats of a single encoding from that stream?"

"Yeah."

"Impressive." His eyes return to the scene unfolding on the viewport. Our hired crew of thirty motley skiffs and frigates spreads into a loose cloud around the renegade planesgate, taking positions. "Are they from consistent sources?"

I run a filter on the packets bursting through local space. "Yeah," I say. "They come from the same four ships."

"Which four?"

"Eaton Tower, General Spinale, Easy Rider, and the Whoop, There It Is."

Blue squares flash bright against the black of his pupils.

I see four messages beam at the four ships. "What are you sending?"

He doesn't answer, so I just look at them myself.

They're lists. The names of outfits that have it in for us: the Black Suns, the Rococo, the Seven-Sevens. The message says we're planning an immediate pre-emptive strike against their dormworlds, and that we leave in less than five minutes.

"What are you playing at?" I say.

The messages contain ten names overall, each with a different combination of a few. There's some design at work, here.

Stroph doesn't blink. He asks, "Are any of them sending a transmission?"

I stare at the feeds. "Yeah. Spinale and the Whoop, on an emergency tightbeam. Megawatt broadcast."

"I see."

He waits five minutes.

Then he launches four tactical nukes signed with an IFF and watches them spiral toward their distant targets. The four ships are swallowed by white-hot spheres, pinpricks in the distance.

Stroph gets onto the broadcast loop. "We caught our moles. They were working for the Kindred Spirits. We are going to hit them back in the next five minutes."

Green lights ping on the consoles. He dismisses them.

"How could you tell who they were working for?" I say.

He adjusts three knobs and warms up the aft guns.

"There were four ships. And there are ten organizations likely to work against us." I nod along. "Four ships give us four bits of information. Sixteen binary strings, which is more than what we need. Do you understand?"

"No."

"For each ship, I can either send them the name of an enemy or I can withhold it. For the Black Suns, I can send it to just the Eaton Tower and that's a one-zero-zero-zero. For the Rococo, I can send it to the Spinale and the Easy Rider—"

"And that's zero-one-one-zero." I'm following, but just barely.

"The moles would've sent out an emergency transmission if they saw a message with their employer in it. When they did, the true binary ID was made clear. The Kindred Spirits, ID zero-one-zero-one—"

"The Spinale and the Whoop."

"Precisely."

The mind on this guy. For months, I had assumed that he'd learned that little trick from some old textbook, but then I spent enough time with him to know that he'd thought it up on the spot.

That's how I know he's sending me a message right now.

I just have to figure out what.

First I focus on the number.

1.752 million.

Was that a pointer to something else? Stroph knows I've got a freakish memory—something in my cells binds to neural tape like a vacuum weld.

One seven five two.

Not the tailcodes for any of the ships we lifted. It wasn't a weapon model, not even a spec number for a replacement part. It didn't match any object I could think of.

I think about what it *means*. It was revenue for our first year of partnership: 118. What else happened in that year?

The Razoukas job. Made us legends. I memorized every passphrase to a Rococo planesgate and Stroph came up with a wild route that had us heist eighty tons

     PRISONER'S DILEMMA ON GLIESE-581C

of cargo in less time than it took them to rotate their codes.

What else?

We sold the Sentillion 'cause it cost us more money than it was worth. And then when Zagran wouldn't sell it back we rolled in with a hardcase full of loaded carbines and shot the place through with smoking holes.

The stills bled frothing gin and I dragged Stroph through juniper puddles while he landed shot after shot after shot, 'till we finally hit the big boss' office, held him at riflepoint, and won back our deed.

Could've died, that time.

Could've died plenty of times.

And that was just our first year together—we were just getting started.

I let the memories fill those empty spaces in my brain. They're warm, laced with adrenaline and fear, with a gold trim of glory. We had a real good run, all told.

But none of it tells me what it means. 1.752 million.

I drift back to the moment we see that number for the first time. I'm kicked back in a hammock with a cig hanging out of the corner of my mouth, watching the smoke drift lazy in the moonlight.

Stroph's by the fire running the numbers. He slides it over onto my display, in big cyan digits written in sans-serif.

1,752,110 kroner.

On our own, we'd barely ever cracked three hundred thou apiece. But just one year together and we had more than doubled our take.

And it only got better.

"Very fruitful," Stroph says.

The smoke curls against the indigo sky.

"Yeah."

I land back in my concrete cell.

That's it. That's what he's trying to tell me. We're worth more together than we are apart.

Five years in prison isn't much, compared to the rest of our lives together. Stroph is telling me he's going to stay silent. We're going to stick together.

The days burn down.

Officer Murph slips his key in the door every evening and every evening, I tell him no.

"This is your last chance," he says.

I'm not sure why I feel so confident. It's always possible this is a galaxy-brained con to get me to keep my mouth shut.

But I still don't say a damn thing, even though I know this might be the last choice I ever make as a free man.

The cop shakes his head and the door clicks closed.

※

The dumbwaiter sinks, sending me like cargo toward the core of the planet. The heat is more oppressive than the gees, and the sweat off my brow steams as it drips onto the creaking, lurching metal cage.

Dust gets in my lungs long before the dumbwaiter spews us into the Orfann Prison intake tunnel. They take my clothes, my rings, my lenses. They run their hands all over me and stick gloved fingers where I desperately don't want 'em. The delousing mist is a stinking stinging fog, with all the other naked silhouettes hunched over like alien shadows cast on a bog-green wall.

They hose us down, give us our prison grays, and send us blind and stumbling into the bright subterranean cavern. It's perpetually lit by a massive white column of argon and mercury-vapor—a cylinder sun that will slowly but surely make us lose track of the days.

It'll make the years go by quicker. Or slower. It's hard to tell.

The place is so big I only run into him after my seventh sleep. Stroph's gnarled in the double-gee, curled up against a wall of red granite. He looks up with that cold, unfeeling face, but I see the recognition in his eyes.

"Good to see you," he says, voice flat.

I know he doesn't *feel* it the same way I do, but I gather him up and give him a tight hug, half-squeezing and half-carrying him as his knees buckle under his own weight.

I'm going to protect him in here.

By the end of the month we're going to be running this place.

I let go and he stares at me with that same impassive face. His eyes aren't wet like mine are. His heart isn't soaring like mine is.

I know that.

But this is a man who looked at the long arc of our lives, and made the call that a half-decade in an underground prison was worth the rest of our free years *together*.

If that's not friendship, then I don't know what is.

"Did you memorize the layout of the cavern and the intake tunnel?" he says.

"Every detail."

"And what of our compatriots?"

"I know names and gang affiliations of everyone in the block."

"Impressive."

He rests against the rock, that big head full of spinning gears.

"I have some ideas," he says.

I sit next to him and stare out into that miserable mass in the middle-distance, all milling about and muttering to each other in the oppressive heat. I skip a pebble across the pavement and turn to him.

"Let's get to work."

PRISONER'S DILEMMA ON GLIESE-581C

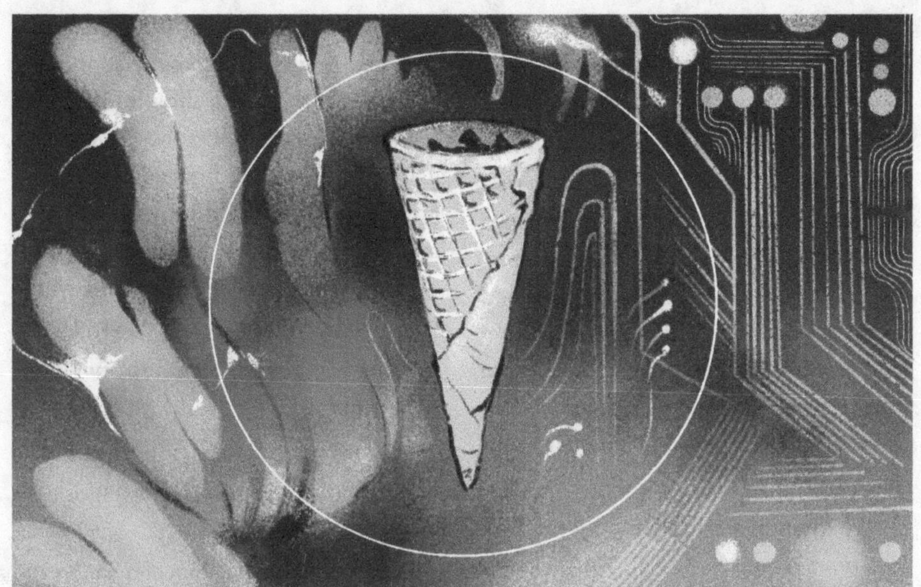

ANAEA LAY

SALAMANDER PATTERNS

I hadn't meant to become an astronaut, but these things happen. I worked hard, because I liked working hard, and that's just where I landed. Apparently a chemical engineer with a PhD in molecular physics and a half dozen Iron Man trophies is overqualified for most other jobs. I'm not complaining. Not meaning to become an astronaut and not wanting to be an astronaut are two entirely different things. Sometimes people don't understand that when I try to explain, though.

Which makes explaining the salamander even harder.

I stretch out on the bed and stare up at the ceiling. It's one of those textured ones that was so popular in the '90s, big lumpy bumps forming random shapes, like constellations in the night sky. They're all familiar. I spent my childhood staring up at that ceiling.

"What do you see?" I ask the salamander grafted to my neck.

"Are you testing my capacity for human-style imagination?" it asks.

"No," I say. "I'm testing your ability to impose meaningful patterns on random data."

There's a shift in pressure at my throat that makes me swallow. The salamander is looking around, pondering.

The blob-shape on the ceiling I'm fixated on has always presented two possibilities to me. In the first instance, it's a woman with her hair pulled up in a bun; it's an old fashioned sort of bun—pulled up, so the hair is big and poofs out from the head before coiling into a spiral that takes up the whole back of her skull. She doesn't have a mouth, but her nose sticks out in a long point.

If I squint the other way, then it's an ice cream cone.

"You don't like this room," the salamander says. "You have strong negative associations with it. Your response to it is one you interpret as claustrophobia."

"That's not something you see. That's something you feel," I say.

"But I do see it. It's a part of trying to see what you see. You aren't actually finding patterns anymore, but recalling past associations."

That's probably true. "And?"

"It's an ice cream cone."

I smile. I'm glad it sees the ice cream cone instead of the mouthless woman. I don't know why.

There's a light tap on the door and I hear my dad's voice. "Sharon? Dinner."

"Coming."

I'm thinking of the ice cream cone and what the salamander said about me, just remembering old patterns I'd found, as I go downstairs and take my seat at the table. I'm sitting in the chair farthest from the kitchen, my back to the patio doors, just like I always did growing up—and have continued to do on visits home to my parents. I do this even though it puts an empty chair to either side of me, where my siblings, who are not here, used to be.

"Did you have a nice nap, sweetie?" my mother asks.

"I wasn't napping," I say. "I still can't nap." Thirty-three years old and I have never napped.

"Oh," Mom says. Then she smiles too big and makes her chair squeak horribly as she scoots in.

"How did your appointment with the doctor go?" Dad asks.

It was terrible. The doctor had started off by consoling me about the salamander, then dove right in with possibilities for removing it. "Humanely, of course," he'd said when he paused long enough to hear my protests.

Never mind that what I had been protesting was the idea that I needed consolation, or that the salamander should be removed. I'd sat there for twenty minutes in the scratchy gown with the confusing ties. Then I told him I'd have to think about what he'd said before I made any decisions. All the while, the salamander sat docile on my neck, never saying a word in defense of itself.

"It was fine," I tell my dad.

SALAMANDER PATTERNS

"Any...news?" my mother asks.

I blink at her, my fork stopped halfway between my plate and my mouth. She is clearly referencing something—and expects me to know what—but I have no idea.

"What kind of news?"

"From the doctor. About Sally."

My mother refers to the salamander as Sally. A doctor on one of Mom's talk shows said we should try to treat the salamanders the way we would treat humans and develop positive relationships with them. He said it's better for those "afflicted" with accidental grafting. As if this is something that happens routinely.

Salamanders are not just like humans. They do not conceptualize themselves the way we do, and they find our self-conceptions peculiar and unsettling. Also, Sally is a stupid name.

"I'm not having it removed," I say.

My mother drops her fork to the table, its tines clattering as they bounce off of the edge of the plate. "Don't you want it removed?"

This argument again. We've been having it for as long as I can remember. Not always about removing the salamander— it's only been a year—but about my failure to do, or be, what they think I should want to do or be. Our relationship was supposed to evolve past this when I moved out, when I became an adult. It didn't, but at least I'm on comfortable footing again. I know how to have this argument.

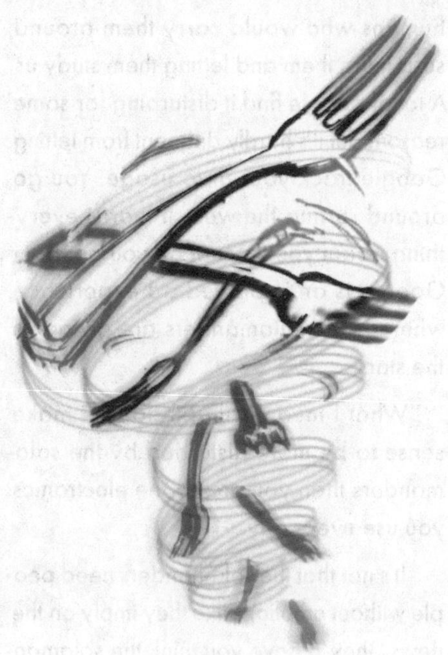

I stick my fork into the pile of noodles on my plate and twist. "I have a responsibility," I say as I pull a be-noodled fork clear from the rest of the plate. "I'm going to see it through."

"Don't be stupid, Sharon. You're not like those others. You didn't ask for this. Nobody can hold you to those obligations."

"It can," I say. I shove noodles in my mouth. "And it's right here, listening."

My dad cuts in, his tone placating, his fork covered in sauce. "Let's change the subject."

＊

None of modern space exploration would be possible without the salamanders. They came to us and taught us how to make it practical, economical, easy. All they asked for in exchange were hosts, humans who would carry them around, sustaining them and letting them study us. A lot of people find it disturbing for some reason, but it's hardly different from letting Google track your data usage. You go around surfing the web, it learns everything about you. Except all you get from Google is an improved ad experience, whereas the salamanders are giving us the stars.

What I mean is that it doesn't make sense to be more disturbed by the salamanders than you are by the electronics you use every day.

It's not that the salamanders need people without emotions like they imply on the news. They'd have you think the salamanders can only graft onto people lacking in real feeling or empathy. But that's not it at all; they don't need an absence of emotion, but a distance from it. They get overwhelmed by people who get overwhelmed. They need people who can think through what they're feeling, who can experience a thing while watching themselves experience a thing. It's not that they have an antipathy to empathy. They just need a host with a certain amount of detachment so they can maintain their own detachment and watch us.

Can you blame them?

I'm lying on my bed again, staring at the ceiling. A foot away from the mouthless lady/ice cream cone is a lumpy huddle of sheep. They aren't really sheep—they don't look like anything—but one night I couldn't sleep and had counted three hundred imaginary sheep, so I decided to find more tangible ones. That wasn't a pattern I found, but one I imposed. And I remember it, all these years later.

"Why do you come back here, when you dislike it so much?" the salamander asks me.

"They're my family," I say, because it's the only answer I have.

Everyone has problems with their families, but you put up with them because they're family. There is no such thing as a functional family. We all know that, even if half of us make ourselves miserable by trying to be the exception.

"Are you dependent on them in some fashion?" the salamander asks.

"They're the only family I have. I don't get another one."

"Why do you need a family?"

This question stumps me. This happens sometimes, when talking to the salamander. They aren't individuals the way we are, so they're fascinated and confused by social networks among humans, the ways our individuals form collectives. I find I can't explain the function of families to the salamander because I'm so fuzzy on the subject myself. I know that family matters and that mine cares for me—people have been assuring me of both points since I was very small—but I am at a loss to articulate why.

"They provide a critical support network, a reliable fall back for resources and assistance should something fail."

The salamander shifts, pressure moving away from my throat and toward my collarbone. "Like for raising children?"

"Yes," I'm pleased to have found something to offer as an explanation. "Grandparents are great babysitters."

"But you have no children. You have no plans to have children. Why come back here when you don't plan to use the benefits rendered by doing so?"

Because where else was I going to go for my mandatory three week vacation? The last time I'd had a mandatory break was college. Maybe that's what I should tell the salamander: we need family so we have somewhere to go when our professional lives start to fall apart. Before I can say that, I hear a gentle tapping on my door. I sigh, but I don't move. I can already predict the next twenty minutes and nobody is going to be happy at the end of them. "Come in," I say.

"Sharon, can we talk?" my dad says as he comes in the door, his face wearing that I come in peace to be the voice of reason expression he uses whenever he feels trapped between me and my mother.

I sit up, suppressing the sigh I feel coming on. "Sure."

"Your mother means well," he says as he sits down next to me on the bed. "This is very hard for her."

"This doesn't have anything to do with her," I say. "It happened to me. It's my life. This is my decision."

"But it reflects on her. On us." The salamander shifts on my neck.

When it talks, I'm the only one who can hear it, but it still rarely speaks when there are others around. It's an observer, and tries very hard not to influence things as they are happening.

"You think this makes you look bad?"

"We think we wouldn't be very good parents if we weren't worried. You know what those things are. What they need. We want you to be happy. But if you're a salamander host, how can that happen?"

This conversation hasn't quite gone where I expected it to. Discomfort with the salamander, I'd expected. Pressure to pretend the accident never happened, or to make a big deal out of it, I'd expected. But this is something...subtler. I'm not sure what to do with it. "I would be unhappy if I had the salamander removed."

My dad sighs, and I wonder whether he loathes these peace-making conversations as much as I do. "I love you, Sharon. Your mother and I both do. And we'll always support you, whatever you do. But we want what's best for you. So if you don't want the salamander removed, will you do something else for me?"

"That depends on what," I say, always reluctant to commit to anything that I don't understand.

"Talk to somebody. A counselor, or a psychologist, or a priest. Somebody objective. Work through things with them. If you do that, and you still want to keep the salamander, that's fine."

He's certain I'll change my mind. He also knows that I'd never, voluntarily, "talk to somebody." This is one of those impossible situations where, in order to avoid looking like a stubborn, unreasonable person in the face of an absurd expectation, I have to give in to another absurd expectation. He thinks he's being fair, kind. He really does.

I think about trying to explain to him why he's wrong. But it'll be one of those cold fights, where we are both perfectly calm and reasonable, and we'll both walk away hurt and disappointed. My teenage years are a mass of scars from those discussions and attempts. He will not understand and I'll never know whether that's because he can't or because he refuses to. But even if nothing else between us has changed since I was a teenager, I have at least learned that much.

"I'll think about it," I say.

He smiles, pats my shoulder. "That's all I ask."

No, what he asked was for me to either cut the salamander out of my neck or to validate their sense that there's something wrong with me by seeking help for it. But he loves me. He'll always support me. Him and my mother, both.

The thing is, he's almost right.

He looks at me and sees the sole survivor of a devastating accident, physically maimed by the event, and refusing to deal with the psychological trauma. That person probably does need to deal with it. That person probably should talk to somebody. Standing up to that person to make sure they get the help they need probably is the best way to express love and support.

"They don't understand you very well," the salamander says when my father is gone.

The problem is, I'm not scarred, and I wasn't traumatized.

I never meant to be an astronaut, but not because I didn't want to be one. Growing up, being an astronaut meant lots of training for the chance to spend a few days in a tin can hovering in the exosphere, eating terrible food and urging middle schoolers into STEM fields via web-cam. We'd already been to the moon and, when we were being honest, had given up on sending people anywhere else. "Astronaut" just wasn't a career option a practical person would find attractive.

"Your subconscious wanted it," the program director told me when they offered me the job. "You couldn't have a more perfect resume for an astronaut if you'd tried."

This comment irritated me a great deal. He wanted to be an astronaut, and in order to like you, he needed to think that you did too. So he invented a life-long self-delusion for me to make me palatable, and never

SALAMANDER PATTERNS

questioned whether that explanation might make me unqualified for the position.

The director's well-intentioned, irritating quirks aside, I quite enjoyed working for the program. The salamanders claimed they'd come from Venus and, publicly, we let that stand. In the program, we knew it was a lie—their arrival trajectories made no sense with a Venusian origin point—but they didn't try to sell the people in the program on it. Wherever they were actually from, whatever they were actually doing, at this point they were a fascinating species giving us technology we craved and access to the universe, in exchange for consensual hosting by a very small number of volunteers.

Everybody suspected that there was another shoe waiting to drop, but there was little we could do until it did. So we kept our eyes open and learned everything we could.

I'd found a niche I enjoyed, got along well with my colleagues, and looked forward to Penelope's launch. My workload was reasonable, which meant I had time to pursue side interests. That was deliberate. The program wanted us cross-trained as heavily as possible.

To a point.

"You got a minute, Sharon?" the program director asked me one day. He was in his late fifties, too old for a position on Penelope but young and fit enough to fantasize about an exception.

"Sure."

"It's about the application you put in last week. To join the ambassador program."

"What about it?" I asked.

"You need to withdraw it."

I turned in my chair to look at him directly. He liked that from the people working under him, especially women. It made him feel like they trusted him enough to be assertive, and he desperately wanted us to trust him. To like him. To petition the higher brass into giving him his hoped-for exception.

"Why?" I asked. "I passed the psychological exams. I qualify." That I'd even consented to the psychological exams should have been proof enough of my interest in the project.

"That's the problem," the director said. "We don't want the public knowing that one of our astronauts qualifies as a salamander host."

This came as a surprise to me. Up to that point I'd only thought of the benefits to the project, the advantages of having an active salamander with the crew to provide advice and guidance if something went wrong. It had seemed to me like the very sort of thing the brass would want.

"I don't understand."

"There is a word for the people who qualify as hosts. It's not one we want associated with our crew."

I still didn't understand. "What word?"

"Psychopath."

More surprise. "You think that I'm a psychopath?"

In that moment, I could see him remembering our first conversation, reconsidering his assertion that really, deep down, his dream had always been mine, too. I did not like the conclusion he seemed to be drawing. "I think you need to withdraw your application. We won't allow a salamander host onto the crew."

I spent four days thinking about it, then withdrew.

Of course, something went wrong. We hadn't even launched yet and the engines were sending up warnings. We delayed the launch an hour to troubleshoot them. Thirty minutes later they were cycling out of control. The evacuation alarms sounded ten minutes later. We'd drilled for a four minute evacuation. The explosion came at one minute-thirty seconds.

I'd taken up post near the salamander storage facility on the ship since none of my skills were useful for troubleshooting the engines; I could contribute best by staying out of the way and monitoring conditions in areas the rest of the crew weren't in. That was what saved me from dying in the initial blast.

I was still a goner, except that the salamanders had been blown out of their storage, too. One of them crawled toward me, the long, tapered appendage that served as an arm and looked like a tail coiling around it when it reached me. Then it tickled my ear.

"We can save each other," it said. "Will you host me?"

I didn't need to think about my answer.

And the merging? Nothing in the universe would convince me to give up that experience.

I miss my crew mates. And I'm sorry the mission failed before it ever launched. Six months of recovery from my injuries was intensely unpleasant. But I wasn't traumatized by the accident.

It gave me the stars in a way success never would have.

I agreed to talk to a counselor.

There were another two weeks left in my enforced vacation, and it was that or leave my parents early. My siblings were coming for the weekend. It would have been awkward, complicated, and needlessly dramatic. My siblings didn't deserve to walk into that. I did insist on a counselor, not a psychologist. I'm not going near anybody who has the authority to do anything.

Her office is drab and plain. Dr. Geffston. Beige berber carpeting and faded chairs with worn padding. No fish tank, but several ficus plants. Neutral-warm smile as I sit down across from her.

"How is Sally?" she asks.
"Who? I'm Sharon," I say.

Dr. Geffston points to her neck. "The salamander."

"The salamander doesn't have a name," I say. "And it doesn't want to be discussed. It's an observer. It doesn't change anything."

"And you're sympathetic to that?" the doctor asks.

My patience for this is shorter than I thought it would be. Already, I want to be anywhere else, and care less about the consequences than I should. "Since you've already spoken to my mother, it shouldn't be hard for you to realize that the problem is her inability to accept that my choices aren't about her. Why don't you have her come in and tell you all about Sally?"

Dr. Geffston doesn't react. I wonder how many of the people chosen to be salamander hosts have training like hers. Is she actually detached, or just faking it to be professional?

"I may do that," she says. "But while you're here, let's focus on you. This isn't the first time that you've talked to someone like me, right?"

No. "I was an astronaut. We have to talk to lots of people like you to get, and keep, that job."

"And before that?"

Before that, I was eight. "I don't see how that's relevant."

"Tell me a little bit about what it's like to host the salamander."

I'm relieved she changed the subject, and I'm sure she notices. "It's not like anything. I mean. Nothing's different."

"Really?"

"Nothing with me. Other people are different. They treat me differently. For the first six months I wasn't sure whether it was the accident or the salamander. I think it was both."

"And now?"

"Now, obviously, it's the salamander. The accident was a year ago." I roll my shoulders a bit as the salamander shifts at my neck.

"In what ways are people treating you differently?"

"They worry about me so much I have to come here to calm them down."

Dr. Geffston has a tablet resting on her lap, but she isn't using it to take notes. I wonder what the point of having it out is. "But they have worried about you like this before."

The sigh escapes before I can stop it. I start to cut it off, then reconsider. It's like a hiccup mid-sigh. But that's all I need to reach my decision. "There's no point to this," I say. "Thank you for your time."

"Sharon!" she calls as I reach the door.

I put up with a lot for the program. I was getting the stars in exchange. But this? There's no reward for this.

I can't face going home so soon. I go to a food court instead, scarf around my neck to hide the tell-tale lump from the salamander. Milkshake, French fries, and cheesy pop music over hollow loudspeakers. It's a sort of hell, really. I haven't been to a food court since high school but, for now, it's better than the alternative. I eat the fried potatoes and wonder whether I ought to regret walking out, whether it was worth the pique of temper. The aftermath of getting angry always leaves me a little afraid.

"Can you take me away from this?" I ask the salamander.

"It is unlikely they will restart the project. And if they do, it is unlikely they'll allow you to crew it," the salamander replies.

These are things I know already. The French fries are too salty and I adore it. "What about...how it was when we merged?"

"I don't understand why you came back here," the salamander says.

It has ignored my question. Salamander tact. "I didn't have anywhere else to go. And I hadn't been home since before the project started. I was overdue."

"You owe them visits?"

"Something like that."

"And what do they owe you?" Love. Support. Understanding.

"Nothing."

"Yet, you honor the obligation. You're unhappy, but you make no effort to change that."

I look at the food, the plastic table, the laminate flooring. It ignored my question and I noticed. If I ask again, will I get an answer? I suspect not.

Salamanders don't go backward.

I remember the first time I saw the mouthless woman on the ceiling. I was six. We had moved into the house just a few weeks before. I stared up at the ceiling from my bed, watching the morning sunlight crawl across it, and wondering whether it was late enough for me to get up yet. I've never slept much, and even then I knew that trying to keep up with me exhausted my parents. So I held still, looking to the ceiling for my amusement, and there she was. I spent a good while wondering whether I'd ever be able to scoop my hair into a bun like hers. I wondered whether her nose had always been so pointy, or if she'd gotten herself into trouble like Pinocchio.

A few years later, I made up a backstory for her. Laying in bed, two weeks after I punched Jimmy Calton for stealing my best friend's Lisa Frank folder. I was scared because the doctor told me that if I didn't control my temper he'd take me away from my family, send me to a school for other kids like me. I didn't know how they'd be like me, just that what I was was horrible, and that the other children would be as well.

So I didn't think about the doctor, or Jimmy Calton, or my parents whispering furiously when they thought I couldn't hear. The lady on my ceiling was a mom, a new mom. She loved her little baby too much for words. Bad fairies were jealous and they cursed her, taking away her mouth so she could never even sing her baby a lullaby. But she loved that baby anyway, even if she was cursed. She loved that baby so

SALAMANDER PATTERNS

fiercely that even without a mouth, even with her pointy nose, she'd never let anybody take it away ever.

I never found her baby.

I don't take off the scarf, and I don't talk about Dr. Geffston. I go out as much as I can, though I have no friends and no connections in this place. I just have to take it one day at a time, and then it's over. I'll wait three more years before coming back, and just stay for a week next time. Maybe things will be better by then. Maybe next time, it'll go differently.

My siblings arrive late on Friday, spouses and children in tow. The kids take over the living room as their bedroom for the weekend, and my siblings put down air mattresses in their respective childhood rooms. My sister is jet lagged and disappears to bed before long. My brother's wife does the same, though without the excuse. My brother and I stay up late in the kitchen.

"You'll need tackier jewelry if you're going to wear scarves like that," he says as he pours us a drink. Then he hesitates. "Can you still drink?"

I scowl. "I'm not pregnant. Give it here."

He teases me, holding the tumbler just out of reach, but I step on his foot and he repents. I've missed him, and I can feel the salamander wriggle in response to my sudden awareness of just how much.

"The folks are worried about you."

I sip my drink. "I know."

"Should I?"

"No."

"Didn't think so." He downs his drink, pushes his glass aside. "So is this the sort of mandatory three week vacation where you still have a job at the end?"

I shrug. "Yes, technically. Not sure for how long, though."

"No funding?"

I take another sip. I know that he won't tell anybody, but still. How much should I share? "No salamanders. They're leaving."

"Back to Venus?" my brother asks.

The squirming is somewhat uncomfortable. I take a breath, try to ease the salamander. It's not normally like this. "The hosted ones will stay, but their ambassadors and the ones who have been teaching us are moving on. They don't have the patience to keep teaching us anymore. Either we figure out what happened on our own, or no stars after all."

He refreshes our drinks, though I haven't finished mine yet. "Well, we'll figure it out. How long do you think it will take?"

"No idea. I'm not that kind of engineer."

He nudges me, grinning. "You're just about everything else, though. What's next for you?"

"I'm not sure." I shrug. "Maybe biology. Well, xenobiology."

"You want to study the salamanders who stay?"

"Of course," I say, grinning because I can tell he understands. Not in any way he could articulate. But he gets me. He always has. I don't have to explain the salamander to him, which makes me want to. "We can't go to the stars, but a piece of them came to us. I think it would be nice to take a closer look at that."

"What does Sally think of that?" he asks.

I cringe.

He squeezes my bicep. "Sorry. Our parents are assholes."

I drink to that.

While they are grafted to their hosts, the salamanders see and feel everything their host experiences. The relationship is reversed during the grafting. I didn't just sense what the salamander was sensing right then, its panic over the explosion, its fear of dying alone in the flames, but I got a sense of everything it had seen and experienced, the sum of all that it was.

They'd come from far, far away. Much farther than Venus. They were all the same creature. They're like starfish, where the pieces survive when you cut them off. They can wander around on their own for a bit, but they'll come back eventually. Join again. There is no going home for a salamander, just becoming whole.

I saw the galaxy, the universe, spread whole and fragile and graspable before them. I felt novae burn and explode and knew it was nothing, a mere second of

the cosmic whole, while I would stretch long past it.

I found thousands of little species, planet-bound and frightened of their smallness, their confinement. And I reached out my hand to help them, the ones that could be helped.

I learned the pattern and shape of the universe, rode the crests of its waves, sank deep into its troughs. I tore off pieces of myself to study it closely, intimately, to become lost in the ebb of it before coming back into me.

I became small.

I accepted confinement.

And I woke up to burning. My other pieces of self destroyed. Facing a moment where I would never be me again, would lose the knowledge and experience I'd gained from my temporary sundering.

Found the girl, the woman, the dying creature I might save, if only she'd let me save this small part of myself.

I became alien, and I folded the universe within me. I was happy.

And then I was Sharon, and there was a salamander living in my neck.

"They make you different," says the salamander after my siblings have left. "It helped me understand."

"Good," I say. And I am pleased. If the salamander is beginning to understand, maybe I'm getting closer, too. I pause for

a moment, a pair of socks clutched in my
hands. Then I recall myself to my task, put
them in the bag.

"You're leaving," it says.

"Spending the next two weeks alone
in my apartment won't be so bad. I think
we'll all be happier."

"Could we visit another host?" the salamander asks. It is the first time it has ever
suggested that I do something. The first
time it has asked me for something since
I consented to host it.

"I think that would be nice." I'm standing on my bed, neck bent to look up at the
ceiling, sharpie in hand. "Will you be able
to merge with the other salamander?"

"No," it says. "But we can share what
we've learned."

It is awkward to draw on the ceiling, my
wrist is bent at an uncomfortable angle, but
it only takes a few strokes and I am finished.

"It's not an ice cream cone anymore,"
the salamander says.

"No," I agree, smiling up at my van-
dalized ceiling. And the woman with the
pointy nose and old-fashioned bun looks
down at me, smiling back.

DANIEL I. CLARK

ESCURO + INGUEM

"I found them," said Escuro, "in a population silo outside Shell Dial: four day laborers—drunkards and thieves, I should say—who were also master musicians in an idiom of the early Waterwaste."

Inguem raised an eyebrow but said nothing.

"Their mode relied on improvisation by human players, so if I wished to hear their music, they told me, I would have to contract a private performance." Escuro offered Inguem a modest smile. "Along with their fee, plus twenty percent, they received food, drink, supplements, and temporary lodgings near my Vail. They did not expect such generosity from an Equal,

but I wanted them in good health, both mentally and physically."

Escuro paused again, waiting for Inguem to guess at his plans. When he did not, Escuro continued undaunted. "Consider, Inguem: in such an ensemble, each performer must anticipate the others. This requirement, I theorized, would tend to foster, even in otherwise unremarkable men, some level of precognitive ability. Would it not be possible, I asked myself, to amplify their collective clairvoyance using an ideo-pharmakon? I thought it would."

Inguem massaged his temples, eyes half-closed while Escuro spoke. Then he took a sip from his tonic and set the glass back down on a side table before looking at Escuro with a pointed expression. "Did you have any notion," he asked, "what the result would be?"

"My hypothesis was threefold," replied Escuro. "First, that even a routine performance would cause the future to impinge on the present to a minute but measurable degree—creating a 'ripple' in the proverbial river of time. Second, that in the case of a performance augmented by the drug, the ripple would become a larger disturbance, a 'wave' sensible to bystanders. And third, that the wave, instead of dissipating its force in the normal flow of time, would propagate itself further into the past."

"No notion, then."

"To test my hypothesis, I recorded their performance covertly. But it will spoil the effect of my story if you insist on understanding right away."

Inguem made a conciliatory gesture, and Escuro began in earnest.

Late in the Sixth Octave, when the Earth had attained Status, and all bonds were loosed, and freedom was all-encompassing, Escuro made a proposal to Inguem.

"By birthright," he observed, "we will live indefinitely. Our welfare, and that of all the Earth, is ensured by Status."

Inguem allowed that this was true.

"Only one thing," declared Escuro, "can relieve the tedium of such an existence, and that is designing or discovering novel sensations." Inguem was of similar mind.

"Then let it be our joint enterprise," Escuro concluded. "With each endeavoring to outdo the other, then both will benefit. The arts of earlier ages, lost technological byways, self-modification regimens of the most esoteric kind—from every one of these we will suck out the marrow."

In this way, Inguem had been persuaded, and after many cycles of slow refinement, their rivalry settled into a comfortable shape. At every new moon, one of the pair hosted the other, assuming two responsibilities: first, to provide accommodation; and second, to produce a marvel.

That role now fell to Inguem, and in six circles he would welcome Escuro to his Vail. His servitors prepared for the impending visit—arranging flowers, polishing display screens and game surfaces, coordinating staff attire—while Inguem, elsewhere among his many rooms, inspected the remains of his midday meal with mingled pride and disgust.

For the past calendar, Escuro and Inguem had made cuisine their study. They kept no strict tally, but Inguem believed that the contest favored him at present. His last showing—a calliopander from the Marble Sphere, served raw in a suspension bath of cold sauce—had been a coup, whereas Escuro's previous effort—a hastily-arranged seance at which semi-substance was to be the main course for both petitioners and guests alike—had produced only vague and contradictory apparitions scarcely worth the considerable effort that went into evoking them.

But complacency would not do.

Inguem stood up from the table and walked to his study. He would likely work on his go rhythm, an autogenerator of recipes in the style of Ronse, esteemed dietician and Equal of Pre-Conciliar Drytime, until the very moment when Escuro arrived for its demonstration, but already he had begun to feel the discontent that invariably accompanied the completion of a work. He was examining this sense of dissatisfaction from every angle, testing it—now seeking to soothe the rancor it kindled within him, now to inflame it further, the better to taste its particular qualities—the notes of bitterness, the tang of resentment and regret—when the wall opposite him flashed red, gold, red.

He sighed at the intrusion but set down his tools and optioned audio only, listening for the sour baritone of his delightful, insufferable friend.

"Inguem," said Escuro with characteristic insouciance, "prepare a chamber for me. I will arrive in two circles, and I will have my phonode with me."

"Music, Equal Escuro?"

"Music, Equal Inguem. I've prepared a recording for our contest. I did not contribute to the performance myself, though you may say that I acted as regisseur. But attend! I will arrive in two circles. You will hear the recording in precisely three."

Strictly speaking, the arrangement that Escuro described would violate the terms of their contest: he was not expected at Inguem's Vail until evening, and the duty of exhibition belonged to Inguem, not him. Inguem mentioned these facts to Escuro.

"You will prefer to hear the recording at home," insisted the latter.

The wall flashed red, gold, red then returned to its default setting.

Wondering at his friend and adversary's cryptic comments, but anxious that his present work not be derailed, Inguem sent a subthought concerning Escuro's early arrival to his majordomo, then once more gave full attention to the go rhythm. The last course and the dessert, on reflection, had lacked the sharpness and immediacy of the other dishes: a few adjustments would suffice to correct the deficit.

A circle elapsed, and Inguem paused to examine his labor. Despite his earlier qualms, he felt a rising excitement as he glimpsed the full realization of his object and allowed himself to consider the possibility that he might add another triumph to his private reckoning of worth.

But remembering what Escuro had told him, he was vexed.

Had they not already spent a kilocycle researching and recovering the music of earlier eras? They had—modifying themselves along the way to become past masters of every extent musical instrument, and reconstructing, along hypothetical lines, those that were lost. The best efforts of a thousand cultures littered their brains.

Had they not spent another kilocycle or more on experiments with psychoactive compounds and auditory stimuli? Indeed—and the results had been so revelatory that Escuro and Inguem afterwards remained three solcycles in special recovery.

To the shock and consternation of those Equals who were occasional witnesses to their exploits, Escuro and Inguem had engaged in dueling via polyphagia, competitive architetris, spectacle demolition, and other amusements still more recondite.

All of them had paled.

Inevitably, Escuro and Inguem were surfeited. Their perceptions became watery and thin. But impoverished soil may be enriched through a controlled burn of vegetation—likewise, they determined, may the capacity for cultivating fresh experience be restored. And so, when they could no longer fully enjoy their sensory diets, they retired to a clinic at Draes Mor Dei, where practitioners of medoctrine flashed out their memories.

The procedure was not without cost. The residue that nourished new growth also ensured that experiences of a kind earlier sown in the mental substrate could not easily be replanted, the fresh qualia they yielded, even in their first ripeness, tasting subtly of ash. But they were committed to their contest, and no price, even the permanent exhaustion of a field of experience, was too high to pay if the alternative was boredom.

"Escuro has some stratagem in mind," thought Inguem. "He would not otherwise risk repeating himself. Yet I may turn this to my advantage, if I take repetition as my theme…"

A concept now took root in Inguem's thoughts: he would adapt his go rhythm to use a nested grammar negatively applied, not to multiple ingredients in a dish, but rather, to a single musical phrase. The go command would extrapolate a larger composition in reverse, so that the piece concluded with the bare motif from which the preceding complications had been derived.

"And at the heart of this inward-leading spiral, a quote from a composition by Escuro!" Inguem chuckled. "Perhaps one that he now disavows!"

Relishing the piquancy of his own wit, Inguem activated the mental prosthesis that gave order to his overburdened mind and roamed as a thoughtself among the memory galleries where his most valued experiences were preserved.

Here, a jewel of an evening: Inguem alone, pilot of a vessel drifting along the banks of a lightless river as armaments were deployed against the perfect black of the Curtain, each explosion timed to coincide with the chords he played on an organ set into the deck before him, the water splashing against the sides of the boat, the headless cranes in flight over the mud flats, the singing reeds, the smoke at dawn.

And here, another, with Escuro for company. They went on an auditory fast for an entire solcycle, then had broken the fast together in an acoustic chamber by a gradual ascension from the lowest to the most piercing tones, from the most fundamental and throbbing to the purest frequencies at the furthest threshold of audible sound.

Inguem lingered for a moment, then sought memories from an earlier time: their first experiments, which were still accessible to him in a gallery he seldom visited, but had yet to sacrifice to the imperatives of the contest. Inguem summoned a face prompt: "Retrieve my musical collaborations with Escuro."

All? inquired the face prompt.

"No," said Inguem, "only those records that date between Ninth and Eighth Eight."

The face prompt flashed green, and a uniq installation began to swim towards Inguem from far out on the endless plane of the Index.

It was a colossal pyramid, partially submerged but rising from the black ground into the carmine of the empty sky; and as an emblem for their explorations during that earlier period, it was an apt choice. Inguem had suggested a traveling show, and Escuro had raised the stakes by insisting—"for the sake of verisimilitude"—on physically transporting the gear and personnel from venue to venue in just such a vehicle as this.

That Vails were customarily separated by great distances was an unfortunate concession to antiquated standards of luxury, both had agreed. Indices had laid open frontiers of inner space that could satisfy even an Equal's desire for solitude, and yet the convention persisted. Both agreed as well that travel was not without its pleasures.

On lengthy voyages down the Glass Coast, over stretches of lost highway, in the shadows of monuments to forgotten politicians, Escuro and Inguem passed the time by sharing rare audio with each other.

One would cue up live books; the other, a satellite synthony; both would say that here was a potential source of inspiration; and the moon would stare down from the black of the Curtain, indifferent.

Your touring transport in replica, stated the face prompt. *It is equipped with a bank of your recordings with Escuro.*

Inguem nodded his satisfaction, and the face prompt winked out. A keyhole opened in the side of the pyramid, and Inguem entered. He ascended to the control booth, where he activated a phonode and set the vehicle in motion.

In the cycles after they had abandoned music for greener fields, Inguem had gradually sold the rights to most of his period-specific muscle memory and sense data to assorted Research Groups and funneled the proceeds into whatever new medium they had selected. Even when they had been active as musicians, Inguem had preferred the ideal composition in embryonic form to the finished piece with its inevitable flaws. Some few master recordings, however, he had preserved, and he sifted through them now as the pyramid trundled across the plane.

"Passable efforts," thought Inguem, "at half-realized concepts."

For a time, he could think of nothing more to add, but in Inguem's heart of hearts a fondness remained for these misbegotten creations; gradually, that feeling rose to the surface. He listened attentively, almost enjoying himself.

From the ghost white office wall—two voices sang in a close harmony—where could I go? I won't pass the physical.

"This is the one," thought Inguem. "Will he recognize the words? If the autogenerator functions as I hope, not until the conclusion of the piece." And he sent an excerpt to be rendered as input for his go rhythm.

An overlay on the viewscreen in the control booth represented the pyramid's movement as two parallel lines converging on the horizon. Inguem watched, but the pyramid came no nearer to the mountains pasted onto the sky at the gallery's edge.

"The symbolism is facile," mused Inguem, "but... compelling."

Now was not the time to give a hearing to doubt, with Escuro soon to arrive.

He optioned null sense.

Cut free from bodily perception to seek refuge still deeper in the vastness of the Deictic Interior, where sensory faculties became invalid and only abstract ideation was possible, Inguem selected one of the Diurnal Mantras, put a language node on repeat, and immersed himself in the purity of the Unspoken Word.

The Interior was a non-place: not a dry grassland divided by sunken rivers; not a tower set sideways, without beginning or end; not an empty room with a distant ceiling and no doors, into which he alone could trespass; not a vast bowl with sloping sides that slowly curved down, down to Inguem, at the center of it all.

In the Interior, Inguem was not-Inguem.

A constant wind passed over him: this was the wind of thought, and only by its touch was not-Inguem sustained in awareness apart from, yet within, Inguem.

The Unspoken Words were carried on the wind. Inguem listened and did not hear.

A scrap of half-remembered melody was picked up by the wind and tossed this way and that, seeming to change shape as it turned and spun, now a cat, now a jellyfish, now a flowering vine, now a—

The melody vanished. Inguem was perplexed: "A filter leak? Wear on the Index? Or an intruder." He thought again of Escuro's call; perhaps this last possibility was one he ought more seriously to consider.

"But that is nonsensical." Inguem slowed his mind. "Not here, where I myself hardly exist. An intoxicant?"

The melody returned. It was a thing of perfect simplicity, wanting nothing but to be heard. Inguem yearned to oblige it.

"This cannot be hallucination!" thought Inguem.

No, this was nothing at all like the chemical deliriums they had once concocted;

ESCURO + INGUEM

and besides, how could Escuro have adulterated his air, food, or water supplies? And by what other manner might Escuro have introduced an intoxicant into his Vail?

The notes ran in sequence, rose and fell, rearranged themselves into playful figures; they made a fugue of Inguem's thoughts, and he laughed.

Still laughing, he found himself in a lush jungle. To his right, his pyramid was visible over the canopy of the trees. "Then I will not be late!" thought Inguem. "It is not too late, the pyramid will get me there before the concert is finished."

He discarded his clothing. A costume grew around him, weaving its tones into themes, and its themes into patterns, as he moved: the result was a kind of dance. With Inguem again at the controls, the pyramid resumed its stately pace.

"A place marvelous strange," observed Inguem. "Terminal, unending afternoon... thunder crackling in the sky... luminescent bugs blink and winged Warnings flutter in the shade. I must try to avoid eye contact... but their beauty is a terrible lure."

The ceiling blazed with heat and light. Inguem wiped the sweat from his brow.

The music listened where it could not be seen. Inguem felt its presence like a soft voice at his ear. Tones flitted between the leaves, leapt from branch to branch, skittering away as Inguem's pyramid plunged deeper into the thick vegetation; the lissome trees were shifting their roots, every motion subordinated to the dance.

Here in this jungle, Inguem would deliver his magnum opus to the world: a masterwork of intricate craft would germinate within him, and yet it would be as new for him, and as fresh, as it would be for the gathered crowds.

It would be a score that was simultaneously both map and territory; a script that wrote itself fluidly, an unstoppable current that shaped all before it in time. The music itself would be his instrument, this jungle and this pyramid as well; and he in turn would be played by the music, each perfectly responsive to the other—all in time, in perfect time.

Sprays of flowers sprung up from the floor; and in each blossom, the music percolated. Through each leaf, as through a window, he saw the music looking at him; in every root, his thoughts ran unceasing circuits; the plants pressed upon him, growing ever thicker; their tones bloomed in awful, overwhelming profusion. The living sounds of the jungle assembled in ranks; notes fell from the sky like rain; and Inguem, scrambling to the apex of the pyramid, reached up with his whole self toward the sun in the ceiling.

"Ah!" gasped Inguem.

Beads of sweat on his forehead were blinding hot flowers, memories wrapped around memories, rippling in the heat, gracefully, like leaves stirred by the wind, honeyed music dripping from his ears, behind his eyes, through his mouth, in every channel and pathway.

Inguem could have been content, had he been allowed to stay.

The majordomo admitted Escuro into Inguem's study, where they found him unresponsive on the floor. Escuro sat in a chair by the window and whispered assurances to the majordomo, who left the room and returned a moment later with the tall cool drink Escuro had requested.

After a circle elapsed, Escuro issued a command to the phonode. Music—first, a trembling drum tattoo, then plangent chords, and hovering over them a sinuous motif—filled the room.

"They rehearsed interminably," said Escuro, "while I increased the dose by degrees. But when I listened to the recording of their final performance, captured at the peak of their synchronization, I was entirely unimpressed. It seemed no more or less than the ensemble's usual fare, and the ideopharmakon I took to be a failure."

Inguem nodded, a wry expression on his face. "Even as the music pierced my awareness and the trance was broken, I couldn't help but think it somewhat..."

"Tepid."

"That is the word." Inguem settled back in his chair. "Perhaps, for us, the result must always fall short of the inspiration."

Inguem fell silent. Then his face flushed, and he rebuked Escuro. "You might come to the point more quickly than you do—

and you certainly could have rescued me sooner! A full circle must have passed before you activated your phonode."

"I might have," replied Escuro, "if rescue had been my intention. It was not. You are still recovering, Inguem, and have forgotten what I said about entering the recording in our contest."

Finding the musicians to be coarse-mannered when not engaged by their craft, Escuro quickly tired of their company. With regret at what might have been, he shelved the recording and put the whole affair from his mind. Jeck, Malwise, Burnton, and Lorge were sent back to their population silo, and Escuro endured the agonies of boredom as only one blessed and burdened with the education of an Equal may.

The matter would have rested there, but a flippant mood took Escuro one evening as he sought, without success, to summon his muse. Deciding that one of the Sequals on his staff might enjoy what he could not, Escuro called for his seneschal.

The man—a solescent, as the unfashionable skin he wore made plain—appeared with customary swiftness.

"Valentun," said Escuro, "I wish to make you a gift for your years of service."

"Yes, sir," said Valentun. "I am grateful, sir. May I inquire as to the nature of the gift?"

"You are familiar with compositional vernaculars of the Waterwaste? No? This will be quite a novelty, then. It is a recording. The phonode is activated by—"

Valentun shrieked. Escuro had not suspected that Valentun was capable of such profound gratitude. He waited for his seneschal to compose himself.

Valentun paced the floor with his face in his hands, still howling. Perhaps this was not gratitude, but fear?

Escuro had no prejudices against religious belief, but also no knowledge of any tradition among Sequals that taught a horror of music.

Not fear, but pain? Escuro was ill-acquainted with physical discomfort. A congenital defect or a faulty audiopatch might account for Valentun's sensitivity, but as Escuro reluctantly conceded to himself, the plain fact was that one could not employ a man who suffered in this way. "A regrettable loss," thought Escuro. "He was... many things to me, I should think. Later I will consult my Index, but first, to business."

He ordered his servitors to place Valentun comfortably in stasis, then put in a call request to the practitioner Kesfick, who had studied at Academy with an Equal of Escuro's acquaintance, and whose other references were impeccably well-maintained. Alone in his study, he activated the phonode again, but as before, the music left him unmoved.

The practitioner Kesfick arrived within the circle. Escuro described to him the circumstances surrounding Valentun's seizure, and the practitioner responded by affirming the diagnostic power of medoctrine, prescribed by just authority. Then he inquired regarding the phonode, and Escuro offered it for his inspection. Kesfick did not activate the recording; nonetheless, he cocked his head, as though listening to something. For some time, the practitioner ruminated, forgetful of his surroundings; but Escuro was well-rehearsed and held the pose indicated by medoctrine—Most Dutiful Patient—without any sign of fatigue.

"I will run the tests personally, Equal Escuro," said Kesfick, returning to himself. "This will take considerable time. Are you prepared to fund my efforts?"

"Yes, of course," replied Escuro, "within reason. I confess that I am not familiar with the expenses involved."

"They are considerable."

"Ah," said Escuro, "yes."

"But the results of such a study!" enthused the practitioner. "I recall the great work of the man under whom I read medoctrine, Director Grafh, who spoke often about the possibility of curatives that might heal past injuries, even those suffered not by the individual but by his antecedents—and the likelihood that remedies of this kind would require a wound sufficiently grievous to resound through the deep time of the body. I hope you do not think the concept macabre?"

To Escuro's great relief, the practitioner absorbed himself in studying charts projected onto the tabletop by his videome without waiting for an answer. He appeared to strain at an insight; his eyes were glassy, and a tremor convulsed the fingers on both hands.

Escuro offered him a palliative, but he declined.

"Equal Escuro," said Kesfick, tapping erratically on the table as though typing a report, "Equal Escuro, what you describe in the case of your seneschal could provide the germ of such a remedy, just as the blue mold produced penicillin!"

He fixed his gaze again on the charts.

"Already the data is singing to me!" said Kesfick. Then he collapsed to the floor, a look of radiant anguish frozen on his face.

"This farce continued for some time," admitted Escuro. "Another was stricken, and another. The restorative effect of playing the recording became clear to me only after seven had succumbed."

Inguem listened impatiently as Escuro explained his surmise: instead of producing a 'wave,' the intrusion of future into present facilitated by the ideopharmakon had created a hollow or cyst in which a creature or force now resided.

"Entities of this kind are well-established in the literature," noted Escuro, "where they are categorized as 'nebuphar, agencies subsistent on human memory, imagination, and desire.' The nebuphar that you encountered that was planted, as it were, in the recording—or rather, in the subjective experience of hearing the recording, however distant in time that might be for any individual—has extended itself outward from the seed produced by my experiment. Any conscious intention to listen to the recording will, I believe, bring the nebuphar into contact with the listener."

Inguem nodded, pursing his lips.

"Your syntax, Escuro, is tangled and inscrutable; likewise, your epistemology."

"I will simplify: the nebuphar feeds the listener fantasies in exchange for the attention it extracts from him. The trick is to modulate the distance between listener and nebuphar—as I did, in your case, with my message—before activating the phonode to close the loop. In formulating the intention to listen while armed with the knowledge that it was three circles distant, you were able to approach the nebuphar safely, without ingesting so quickly that your mind was flooded and without your mind giving so much of its own substance that it was emptied; whereas my staff, and that hapless practitioner, all of whom imagined they would hear the recording presently, were overwhelmed."

"You did not experience anything similar yourself?"

"I am immune to it, Inguem; I was present when the recording was made, and it seems my immunity is irremediable."

Inguem sipped at his tonic and waited for Escuro to go on.

"My seneschal could speak only of an infinite string, vibrating along its entire length so that every tone was sounded, ever-changingly. I upbraided the man for his prolixity, of course, but to no avail. Poor fellow! He couldn't have answered my questions, even if he had understood them. Medoctrine prescribed a full flash, to the outer edge of core personality."

Escuro frowned.

"I took the opportunity to change his name. Chahlus is better than Valentun, as you must agree. Perhaps I'll change my own name some cycle."

At last, Escuro was entirely silent.

"What was it like?" he asked.

Inguem considered how to respond—but not quickly enough.

"Say nothing," said Escuro. "I may judge by your expression. Yes, Inguem, I have invented an ecstasy I cannot access. But consult your Index: you will find that the nebuphar has continued to grow. You will find it has grown rampantly."

Inguem blanched as Escuro delivered his coup de grâce.

"Your treasuries, no doubt, are secure, and I trust your simstems are current. But the nebuphar's roots—its shoots, its flowers, whatever you term them—will nonetheless have overwhelmed your general storage."

"I see," said Inguem, taking care to display no further emotion as his Index confirmed Escuro's boast. "Then the jungle was more than metaphor."

"Oh, indeed," said Escuro. "It appears that the memories of the nebuphar are able to reproduce themselves—with remarkable fecundity."

"So," concluded Inguem, "you have presented me with a choice: given their mass, I can preserve the memories in usable condition only if I abstain altogether from novel sensations, disqualifying myself; I can avoid admitting defeat only if I flash the memories, so that subsequent exposure to the nebuphar will fail to produce any effect."

Inguem stood and adjusted his garments. The moment called for graciousness on his part.

"Victory is yours," said Inguem. "You are sly, Escuro. I will not abandon our contest, so I must instead commit another strange beauty to oblivion. Yet I may have anticipated your rapier wit—in fact, I was just finishing with my go rhythm when the fit took me—and I feel even now that some margin remains in which I might scribble before booking my suite at Draes Mor Dei. Would you like to hear my variation on your theme? 'Companion Turns' is the title."

Escuro assented, and Inguem demonstrated his go rhythm, and they laughed together, savoring the acid flavor their jesting lent to a passing moment that was, after all, just another episode in their long, long lives. Then, bidding each other farewell, Escuro and Inguem separately returned to the task of preparing for their next match.

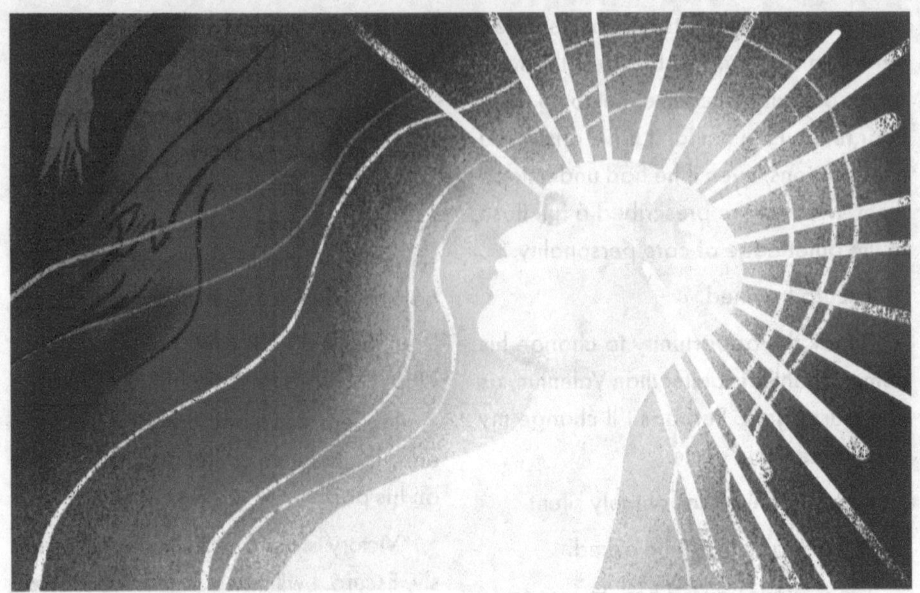

JONATHAN LOUIS DUCKWORTH

THE FOURTH TENET

Even now, I remember the former Chief Auditory Compositionist, Gergus, as a more than adequate crewmember. An auditory compositionist has an important role on a warship—to maintain the systems that produce the sounds of battle, superimposing noise over the tomblike silence of spaceborne engagements. The shrieking *piu-piu* of the point-defense cannons and the booming *thuuwump-thuuwump* of the ship-to-ship disruptor arrays are essential to morale, and what glory would there be in watching an enemy target decompress or disintegrate silently?

I've forgotten to introduce myself. I am Veer, a soldier. At the start of every work span I emerge from my personal sac, wipe its secretions from my carapace, and recite the Three Tenets:

(1) *My Solitude is my Greatest Gift*

(2) *The Hierarchy is Infallible*

(3) *My Silence is my Loyalty.*

Although I now occupy a higher station, for many cycles I was First Adjutant on the Tossi Continuity's glorious warship *Unrelenting Virtue*, where I had served in respectable competence under High Commander Kraalii.

Back to Gergus—they were a better than adequate compositionist in every way but one. They were too pleasing to the eyes and smelled too appealing, like the aroma of the Red Wastes after a rain.

I cannot know what others thought of Gergus, but to me they were an impressive specimen, quite narrow-headed for a compositionist, and rather broad of carapace. A compositionist should be one easily ignored, one who moves quietly in the shadows of the bridge. And yet it was hard not to notice Gergus. That someone so robust and handsome should have been sorted into the compositionist's profession rather than foot-soldier or bridge guard seems strange, and yet I must not question the Hierarchy, nor the infallibility of the same examinations that gave me my station.

The trouble began half a cycle ago, during the early workspans of the campaign against the human scourge. During a battle against a large cluster of New Earth Alliance patrol ships, the compositional systems failed, and the bridge fell silent. Filling the void came a hissing sound, one that I recognized only after a moment, and then with a jolt of terror. Instead of the comforting sounds of battle, from the speakers flowed the sound of someone breathing in their sleep.

It was a sound I had not heard in many cycles, not since the chaotic times of youth before the Great Reordering, before the advent of the Continuity, when I slept in squalor with my broodmates, and some nights I would hear my kin breathing as I watched the stars silently burn above. To hear this, and to be haunted by such memories was a terrible thing. The High summoned Gergus.

"This is your fault," High Commander Kraalii boomed. "Explain yourself."

My rods withdrew into my head, and I know I wasn't the only body on the bridge quaking, and yet humble Gergus seemed unmoved. They stood high on their heel-spurs, a ludicrous show of defiance while being reprimanded.

"I do not understand, High Commander," Gergus said. "How such a malfunction could occur is beyond my comprehension, for I am only a humble compositionist."

The High Commander, to my great surprise, simply ordered Gergus to fix the malfunction, which they did, swiftly, and the *piu-piu* and *thuuwump-thuuwump* returned just in time for the disintegration of the last human ship. And yet despite the triumph, I did not feel the usual elation that follows a victory. In the slumped postures and retracted heel-spurs of the other bridge crew I discerned that the others were left similarly cold. All because of Gergus and their blunder.

In older, more backward times before the Great Reordering, Gergus's mistake would have occasioned much gossip throughout the bridge crew and the rest of the ship. Fortunately, we live in a glorious age where citizens and soldiers are free of the tyranny of community and its virus of conversation, and as every crewmember returned to the unalloyed darkness of their personal sacs at the end of the workspan, Gergus's mishap and the disturbing sounds it summoned would be forgotten.

By all save me. To my great shame I lay awake, my own breathing reminding me of the horrible hiss that had infected the composition speakers. I recited the Three Tenets and the Fifteen Adjunct Sub-tenets to myself sixteen times before the sac's anesthetics settled me to slumber.

I sometimes wonder if my deficiencies—my inordinate interest in the impressions and concerns of others, my heightened awareness of others' moods—stem from the exhausting but necessary duty of a First Adjutant to serve as a bridge between the various hierarchies. As the High Commander's assistant and drudge, a First Adjutant must be aware of all, from engine technicians to weapons operators, bridge guards to supply clerks, and must be prepared to interact with any of them at any time. A First Adjutant and the Second Adjutant below them must pollute themselves this way for the good of the ship.

And so it fell upon me to dole out Chief Auditory Compositionist's punishment: a three-workspan loss of rations. When I summoned Gergus to my office, my assistant, Second Adjutant Shmeel was at my side.

"Lower your spurs in the presence of your betters," Shmeel snapped as Gergus strode in, propped to such tremendous height that they almost scraped the bulkhead.

Gergus did as commanded. "I am sorry, Adjutants. I am a simple compositionist; I often forget these things." Already my carapace itched from the strain of conversation. I waved my lower appendages, signaling for silence, and told Gergus of their punishment.

"The Hierarchy is always right," Gergus said. "I accept the punishment."

Beside me, Shmeel's mandibles ground together with barely contained fury.

"You do not *accept* it. It is simply so," I said.

"Of course, Adjutant."

I dismissed them with great impatience, for at this point I was almost intoxicated with their wet desert musk.

How I would like to say this is the end of my story, and proceed to summarize its lesson. A good story should be short, with a clear moral. I fear this is a rather bad story; such things are not my vocation. And anyway, Gergus's transgressions—and what followed them—would not allow this story to be simple and good.

Several workspans later, during a routine bombardment of a human colony—undefended, as most of them were—in the Tiyanka Shroud, the glory of the sounds of battle were replaced by a grave affrontery. There are few sounds more offensive to the ear-rod than human music. All music is terrible and toxic, but human music is a special kind of chaos. I recognized the horrible whine of the thing humans call a *trumpet*, an obscene brass contraption shaped like a prolapsed ovipositor.

This time, High Commander Kraalii was so rightfully incensed they cut the bombardment in mid-progress and demanded I bring them Gergus.

THE FOURTH TENET

Gergus once more stood before the High Commander without cringing. Again, the High Commander berated them, and again Gergus pled ignorance.

"I could have you demoted," High Commander Kraalii said, shaking their claws, which were twice the size of a commoner's, large enough to easily tear one's carapace open.

Gergus agreed they could do that.

Again, my rods retracted, and my secondary heart swelled with nervous mucus. What was it that Gergus was playing at? There were many lesser compositionists who would gladly ascend the hierarchy at their expense.

Yet, for reasons I did not understand, the High Commander did not remove them. As before, Gergus was commanded to sanitize the composition and restore it, then dismissed from the bridge.

I could not help but glance around at the rest of the bridge crew. Like me, their rods were retracted, and many were venting pheromones, but none as potent as Gergus's accursed musk.

At the end of that workspan, as I went toward my sac in the midnight corridor, I became aware of another presence in the narrow confines of the corridor. There should've been no one there—that corridor was for only a select few officers, and our schedules were set to avoid interactions.

It was Shmeel.

"First Adjutant, we must do something about the compositionist," Shmeel said, their appendages folded over their thorax, their mandibles set in a hard circuit. A small thing they were, with a pebbly carapace and an ugly, broad head.

It was irregular, for a subordinate to intercept their superior on the way to rest. It was not technically a breach of conduct, and yet any sort of assembly, even one between a subordinate and their direct superior, is always suspect. There is invariably pollution in such contact.

I almost didn't answer them—I shouldn't have.

"Yes," I said.

"The High Commander will demand a stern punishment."

Who was Shmeel to say what the High Commander wanted? "Yes, Shmeel."

Shmeel was a purer adherent to the Three Tenets than I, and a harder worker, I must confess. From the moment they were assigned beneath me, I suspected they would displace me. That is the way of the Hierarchy. And yet here Shmeel betrayed a weakness I'd noticed before: an intemperate zeal to distinguish themselves.

An idea occurred to me.

I tasked Shmeel to investigate Gergus, a task they seemed more than eager to carry out. Then, I dismissed them and carried on to my sac where I was insulated from further pollution.

A dull series of workspans followed. I busied myself with ensuring efficiency amongst the ship's various hierarchies, while Shmeel watched Gergus as a broad-wing watches a forest burrower. The High Commander, meanwhile, had retreated ever deeper into their own confidence—a noble practice, to be true, but worrisome for the master of a ship, who must pollute themselves to maintain morale and exert their benevolent influence upon the crew. During those spans I didn't see the High Commander, and only received their communications by writing.

Toward the end of this doldrum, the ship's sound technicians—a separate hierarchy from the compositional array—were testing the ship's warning systems when the usual blaring sound of the alarm was replaced, quite inexplicably, with a strange, woody tapping sound, set in a steady two-three beat. As I stood in a corridor halfway between my sac and the bridge, a memory ambushed me, a musty little mote of mnesic detritus—I had heard this beat before.

To my everlasting shame, my front-facing feet began to tap out the rhythm, while my rear feet—against my will—began to shuffle, and my appendages swayed side to side.

I was not alone. There were soldiers and crew of lower hierarchies—their limbs also moved to the rhythm.

Music has been outlawed because it exerts power over our species' autonomic functions, such that our reputation before the Great Reordering among the sector's other nations was as a race of shiftless, soft-shelled musicians that would

burst into spontaneous dance at the merest drumbeat.

I don't know how long I twisted and writhed at the mercy of my own motor-cortex. A deck guard rescued me and the others by shooting out the emergency speaker with their sidearm.

In the aftermath of the "dancing plague," as the High Commander referred to it, as Shmeel and I were summoned to give counsel. By this time the Chief Sound Technician, a splendidly conventional and loyal soldier named Tyiffix, had already resigned their post and requested a reassignment to a garbage tow, a request High Commander Kraalii granted.

The three of us met in Kraalii's office, a large, spacious room that doubled as an auxiliary munitions storage, as no space is wasted on a Tossi ship. Not like the Thra'ha'khen, who have huge chambers on their ships where their officers weave tapestries, or humans who waste space with tanks of water populated with aquatic creatures.

"The last sound technician didn't understand how it could have happened," Kraalii said. They looked tired, and a thick crust of pale grime had formed on their nasal pores and eye-ridges, a sign they hadn't been cleaning themselves. "The new sound technician determined an invasive subroutine was installed, perhaps as a random glitch."

They said this without confidence, as if they knew very well the truth but could not articulate it. Beside me, Shmeel's mandibles dandled with frustration. It was not for them to speak out of turn, unless I recognized them. I was cruel enough to oblige them, even knowing how it would end.

"Shmeel? You have something to express?" I offered. Shmeel launched into a speech that seemed rehearsed, right down to the emphatic angles their limbs assumed as they pronounced Gergus's name. Gergus had been seen wandering near the sound technician's personal terminal during the previous workspan, and though they had not witnessed Gergus touch it, it was too obvious that they were behind the sabotage. Gergus had to be immediately punished, either with death or else jettisoning.

"You have no proof of this claim, Second Adjutant," Kraalii said, when Shmeel had finished.

Shmeel should have stopped there. I should have stopped them. But they spoke up, "High Commander, it is simple reasoning. Gergus has sabotaged their own systems and now has sabotaged that of the sound technician. They are engaging in a conspiracy to disaffect—"

"Gergus is a compositionist, not a sound technician. Is that not true?"

"Yes, but—"

"Your supposition is based on the possibility that Gergus possesses sufficient mastery of the sound technician's systems to manipulate them, but were that the case, the Hierarchy would have placed Gergus as a sound technician, not an auditory compositionist. Is that not true?"

Shmeel's clever words suddenly failed them.

The High Commander continued, "A weapons calibrator cannot sanitize a sac any better than a sanitizer can calibrate a point-defense cannon—every occupation is as solitary as each individual. The Hierarchy is absolute and infallible, or is that not true?"

Shmeel admitted their mistake, but it was too late.

✳

I saw Gergus among the many grim faces arrayed in the hangar bay, all of us gathered to watch Shmeel's flogging. The public flogging is a holdover from pre-Reordering times, but there is a lucid logic in the pollutive public gathering, that the spectators—forced to see and hear and smell each other—are punished as much as the guilty individual, that they may learn the same lesson.

Gergus hid their eyes when the bridge guards parted the plates of Shmeel's carapace, revealing their translucent vestigial wings and the soft, gummy, nerve-rich meat they folded into. I watched Gergus's ear-rods retract as the lashes—archaic weapons made from the knotted leather of desert crawlers—began to batter Shmeel's exposed nerve tissue. Shmeel shrieked, the sound its own kind of music, and the fringes of the lashes spattered flecks of green ichor on the pristine deck. Was there irony in Shmeel being punished while Gergus remained untouched?

No, not really. Gergus, whether they were incompetent or malignant, had always defended themselves by deferring to the Hierarchy, while Shmeel, in accusing Gergus, had questioned it.

Through all the lashing and screaming, High Commander Kraalii remained an icon of stoic resolve, watching the spectacle with all six eyes unlidded, their ear-rods fully erect.

Seventy lashes in total, each one punctuated by screams that diminished in volume as Shmeel's higher brain functions failed. Toward the end, when more of Shmeel was on the deck than inside their carapace, and the limp tubers that had been their wings lay twitching in green puddles, I began to discern a certain pattern to the lashes—a two-three beat. Did I tap my feet to it, to the sound of my would-be usurper's destruction? I cannot recall.

The rest of the workspan was leisurely. I accepted the services of my new Second Adjutant, the former Bridge Overseer Byar, whose first responsibility was to dispose of their predecessor's carcass in the organic recycler. Afterward I assisted the High Commander in planning the impending engagement with the remnants of the human fleet near Yiikap's Nebula. At the end of it, I retired to my sac, grateful for another downspan of solitude.

But once again I found sleep elusive. The sac's sedatives seemed to have lost their potency, or my body had developed a tolerance. With no chemical recourse, I turned to meditation, and had the sac's internal composition recite the Three Tenets to me. 25 blissful recitations followed. But with the 26th recitation came a new phrase, spliced into the sequence between the third and first tenets: a Fourth Tenet.

Music is the soul's body heat.

I listened, helpless and terrified, as the Fourth Tenet wriggled like a parasite into my ear-rods, into the dark combs and unlighted whorls of my brain, until at last I tore off the sound panel and smashed its transducer. But though I had silenced the blasphemy, breaking the transducer wrought another terrible, unintended consequence. Without the transducer's stream of noise-canceling waves, I could hear outside of my sac—the other, adjacent sacs' occupants, their twitching and their scratching, and I could hear the recitations of the tenets, including the Fourth Tenet, multiplied from every direction.

I still don't know how widely the contamination spread, if it had impacted only the sacs of the midnight corridor or the entire ship, but if it had, there would be no acknowledgment from anyone on the ship. To speak of such a thing would be to speak of the ultimate privacy of one's own sac, to make as great a mockery of the First Tenet as the blasphemous false tenet had.

This was a time of great troubles; many I did not see coming. As a mere First Adjutant I was not privy to the same intelligence as the High Commander, so I didn't realize that the humans, seemingly on their last stand, had received material and technological aid from our rivals, the Kadians, (perhaps because the humans, being of Kadinoid configuration, resemble them), nor that the Thra'ha'khen Empire, perceiving our preoccupation, had launched an invasion of our exposed arm-ward flank. There were other, even more sinister developments on the homeworld to which I was also blissfully ignorant.

All I knew was that the ship's morale was failing, and nowhere was this more apparent than in High Commander Kraalii.

Once a paragon of hygiene, Kraalii was now so filthy with the grime of their sac that their tarsi left little triangular prints of slime on the deck, and their ear-rods twitched at the slightest sound.

Something unwholesome was simmering, and I knew Gergus—the fragrant fiend— was at the center of it. I almost dreaded the next battle, and feared its coming.

But come it did. In concert with *Rigid Adherence and Mindful Penitent*, we had cornered the tattered remnants of the human's fleet at Yiikap's Nebula. It should have been a great triumph, the crowning moment of our long campaign.

Instead, it was a disaster.

At the height of the battle, as the *Rigid Adherence* traded shots with the humans' dreadnought and we and *Mindful Penitent* attempted to head off their cruisers and transports, the *piu-piu* and *thuwuump-thuwuump* ceased, as I feared they would.

I recognized it at once, the warm, round bleat of the bladder-harp, the most ubiquitous of Tossi instruments in pre-Reordering times. Only a few notes were necessary before I felt myself transported through the cycles and through the stages of my life to my nymphal-phase, when I was a dirty savage like the rest of my people.

I was back at the Festival of Three Suns, an occasion that came on the homeworld only once every six spans when the three stars of the Kwimer system synchronized and rose above the Rainshroud Mountains simultaneously, shining their three-hued glory—red, orange, and yellow—on the massed crowds of revelers. I remembered it as a chaotic, sense-blasting spectacle of noise and smells, the throngs so dense that carapaces ground against each other and limbs tangled. So much disease, so much risk of injury, so much *pollution*. Even off-worlders partook, for in those times aliens were not anathema—like soft-shelled fools we welcomed them on our worlds and allowed them to pollute us.

Despite all my training, some disloyal parts of my body still stirred to the bladder-harp's bleat. My secondary heart swelled with mucus, chlorine salts evaporated from my eye fluids, and it took a supreme effort to stop my limbs from breaking into dance right there on the bridge. As the bladder-harp swelled through the composition speakers, we on the bridge were paralyzed, and I could only watch the viewscreen in helpless dismay as the human ships darkened, bent, and then vanished into slipspace.

The battle was over, and the speakers switched off, the bladder-harp replaced by dead silence, and in that dead silence I couldn't possibly fail to detect the susurrus of someone's inner jaws: the Inward Wail.

The Inward Wail is acceptable only during Continuity-sanctioned periods of mourning, such as after the death of a great war leader or Continuity Council member. I turned my head, ready to reprimand the culprit with utmost severity.

But it was High Commander Kraalii. And they were not alone—others, including Second Adjutant Byar and First Pilot Eziik, were also debasing themselves with this unwonted display of emotion.

It was like watching them die. Or their careers, at least.

I alone seemed possessed of my faculties, and I alone had the presence of mind to summon the traitor who had cost us the battle. Gergus appeared, as always, high on their spurs, redolent with that awful, unctuous musk. The only thing that had changed about them since the other incidents was that rather than their carapace shining, it seemed coated with the same sticky grime as covered the High Commander's. A strange coincidence, I thought at the time.

By this time, High Commander Kraalii and the others had composed themselves, and yet—in breach of protocol, but necessary under these extreme circumstances—it fell to me to carry out Gergus's castigation.

"You are responsible for this latest outrage," I said. "You have not only dishonored your post but have cost us the glory of victory with your distraction."

Gergus did not answer at first. They stared listlessly at me, and then at the High Commander. Just as they seemed ready to speak, the High Commander stepped forward, coming between us.

"Deny it," High Commander Kraalii demanded. My second heart, already swollen, began to palpitate.

"I will not deny it," Gergus said. "I have only done what my conscience demanded."

"You dare—" I began, but the High Commander cut me off with a sharp wave of their appendages.

"Deny it, I said." High Commander Kraalii was suppliant now.

"I am guilty," Gergus said. "Guilty of perceiving the truth: that the Solitude is poison, that the Hierarchy is a shackle, and

THE FOURTH TENET

that the Silence is a slide into oblivion. I confess here that I might show those who are like me and who feel alone that they are not alone. *You are not alone.* I accept my punishment, whatever it may be."

I don't blame High Commander Kraalii for staggering and scratching their ear-rods after hearing such blasphemy. They muttered something beneath their breath, and then spoke clearly, "Then, you will be jettisoned."

Mandibles chattered all through the bridge. There is no punishment worse than jettisoning for a crewmember in the Continuity's fleet, for it is a punishment disguised as a reward.

For their jettisoning, carried out that very workspan, Gergus was confined in an escape pod, with its slipspace aperture and navigation terminal both disabled, provided with a limited supply of sustenance, and sent adrift. Before the launch, it fell to me to escort them to their motile prison. They were restrained, their upper limbs shackled together, and their mandibles banded shut, though these measures couldn't prevent them from speaking.

"You are not like the rest," Gergus whispered. I would not speak to a criminal and deviant. "You are different. Like me. Like Kraalii."

"Do not speak of them," I snapped. "You are nothing like us. We are loyal."

"The three of us share a common thread, Veer. We remember how it was before, when our people knew themselves. We haven't forgotten, though we may have tried to."

"Silence. No more from you."

"When we were last joined, meshed together in their sac, Kraalii told me you were another too intelligent to swallow the lies. Maybe there is yet hope for you."

It took three bridge guards to pull me off them, and by that point I had fractured Gergus's mandibles and crushed two of their eyes. Yet the four remaining eyes—the same crimson color as the least of Kwimer's suns—regarded me with a terrible, corrosive sympathy until the airlock sealed shut. This is what haunts me—that they saw me as if I were the one to be pitied.

I watched Gergus's little pod disappear into the black jaws of the universe, and wondered at what point the splendid isolation would give way to the horror of ever direr rationing and the certainty of death.

With Gergus's removal, the *Relentless Virtue* should have returned to normalcy. But High Commander Kraalii seemed a broken machine now. With each ensuant workspan they delegated more authority to me, until such a point that I was, in effect, the true High Commander of the ship. That was not the worst of it. Gergus's corruption had metastasized. Once unheard of, arguments began to break out among the lower orders, some escalating to physical brawls. Incidents of disobedience flared up across every segment of the ship. They were swiftly dealt with, of course, but that they had happened at all disturbed me. In one case, two crewmembers were caught sharing a single sac, and to magnify the outrage, they belonged to entirely different hierarchies—one a sanitizer, the other a logistics clerk.

It was the fifteenth workspan following Gergus's jettisoning when I emerged from my sac to the sound of liquid dripping into a puddle somewhere in the adjacent corridor. I followed the drip's echo to its source, a bulkhead that separated the midnight corridor from the twilight corridor, where lower orders slept.

My organs knotted inside me at the sight of the hideous Fourth Tenet, painted onto the bulkhead with the vivid green of fresh blood. *Music is the soul's body heat.*

I drew my sidearm and resolved to find the culprit and seize justice from them. The desecrator had left a trail of blood in their wake, one easy enough to follow, and even were there no blood I could hear the crack of a lash somewhere deeper in the corridor. Through a maze of pulsing, sweating sacs, I found the saboteur. They stood in a darkened corner, the plates of their carapace roughly torn open, revealing the soft, leaking tissue they'd torn with the lash they now held in a limp appendage.

Their lash was no match for my sidearm. "About face, degenerate," I commanded.

I barely recognized High Commander Kraalii. They had not used their sac in many spans, and they were malnourished, their carapace a mostly empty shell I could see through. Their blood dripped from the lash and from their mutilated wingcase, a sinister music: *plip-plip-plip.*

They staggered past, heedless, as if they hadn't noticed me. I didn't follow them; I couldn't move.

Kraalii resigned their command the next workspan, which—even barring their sedition—would have been its own cause for execution. To resign in disgrace as a High Commander is to make a mockery of the Hierarchy's immaculate mandate.

So now, I am High Commander of *Relentless Virtue.* The glorious war goes on, much to my pleasure. Though they appeared on the verge of collapse, the humans have proved more resilient than expected.

All the more glory to the Continuity.

The new Chief Auditory Compositionist, who is so excellent at their work I can't recall their name—ensures that each engagement erupts with the glorious song of *piu-piu* and *thuwuump-thuwuump* and the eruption of bursting reactor cores and decompressed hulls.

As High Commander I am privy now to the same briefings that Kraalii once received. Gergus spoke honestly when they said they were not alone. Even as our enemies—the depraved humans on one side, the bloodthirsty Thra'ha'khen on the other—close in, on our own worlds there are those who defy the Three Tenets by committing heinous acts of depravity and sabotage. They call themselves the Assemblists, as they demand the right to pollute themselves through free, open assembly.

THE FOURTH TENET

But they will fail. We, the loyal soldiers of the Continuity, will crush these degenerates as surely as we will annihilate our enemies from without. In this my conviction is absolute, even as refugees from the outer colonies pour into the core systems by the hundreds of millions, even as dissension and degeneracy fester and tap their hateful, rhythmic messages within the hull of my ship.

Only in my weakest moments, those fluttering instants in my sac before the sedatives ease me into the downspan, do I think of that archdegenerate Gergus, who has come to represent to me all the serried enemies of the Continuity. The Hierarchy is simple: we are chosen for the role we are capable of performing and nothing more, and so it's impossible that a mere Auditory Compositionist could override the controls on their prison-pod and start up the slipspace aperture. And yet, in these vulnerable moments where I may confuse vice for virtue and grope at fantasies and phantoms, it seems to me Gergus was no ordinary compositionist, and that, if they are alive, our enemies may yet win.

VIOLET ALLEN

INFINITE LOVE ENGINE

Beeblax beats its wings against a superlumic slurry of time and space, and the universe turns to liquid starlight in its periphery; inside rides Aria Astra—Stellar Champion of the Star Supremacy, Wielder of the Sister Ray, Spacetrotting Coolgal, and Humanity's Last Hope—nestled within a blob of translucent pink jellymeat, and it is totally cool and only a little disgusting.

This jelly is Beeblax, or it's at least the material Beeblax that Aria's senses can perceive, or at least the phenomenon of Beeblax that exists in the moment of Aria's perception. And Aria perceives an infinity of Beeblax all around her, a measureless swarm only slightly obscured by jelly and motion, and within each one is a different iteration of herself—every Aria that has or would ever travel with Beeblax in every possible universe, all shooting through the same hyperstream along a single chain of moments, like motes of dust dancing on a sunbeam.

Aria takes a long, sweet snort of it/them. The taste evokes a memory of roses in their platonic ideal, and she enjoys the anagogic tingle of Beeblaxness in her lungs. There is a little piece of her that is afraid—the horny, angry, frightened pig-baby that skulks in the limbic sewer at the bottom of the brain. *You're drowning in slime, babe, it says. Engage complete autonomic freakout.* But Aria is like, *Nah pig. This is chill. Don't fuck this up for me.*

    INFINITE LOVE ENGINE

And she does not let it fuck it up for her. Her breaths are as deep and slow as those with which gods animate universes.

"Still," says Beeblax, continuing a conversation it and every iteration of Aria had been having since like forever. "Like, even if the right glop is out there for me, how am I supposed to know? Am I supposed to become better for them, or am I supposed to stay the same forever so they can recognize me? If we merge into a singular perfect being, will I still be able to hang out with the homies and eat breakfast for dinner? Or will I have to eat brunch? I hate brunch. Brunch is like someone turned eating into a job. I just want to eat breakfast in my underwear."

Beeblax doesn't speak so much as psychically harmonize to the vibration of Aria's soul. It tickles a little, spiritually speaking, but Aria's giving Beeblax serious counsel here, so she keeps her soul from laughing.

"But that's the dream though, right?" she says/thinks. "To find someone with whom to share underwear times, both casual and saucy."

"That's what they say," Beeblax psychically harmonizes. "But there's more to life than kissy face bullshit. Every moment I spend with some glop doing the same old whatever is a moment disappeared into universal nothingness. I'll never get those possible experiences back, right? So even if I'm the happiest I could be, I am still limiting my potentiality. But then again, when it's over, I feel terrible."

"Aren't you a fifth-dimensional cosmic constant? Is lost time really an issue?"

"I'm dumbing it down for you. I feel like we're having some good real talk, and I don't want to glop it up with a lecture on the nature of the universe and/or my existence that would goop up your mindhole. I don't eat brunch either. That's just some shit I stole out of your brain to convey meaning in absence of a shared reference point. Just go with the metaphor."

"That's cool. I'm just saying. I think you're overthinking it. You've gotta just let these things happen."

"I know. I know everything. It's just hard sometimes. The glop of life is long and boring."

Sometimes, another Beeblax will glide over to them, and Aria will see one of her other selves up close. They are mostly all the same, differentiated mainly by affectations: clothes and hair and a few years given or taken. And Aria wonders if the other Arias are on the same mission as she is in their universes, or if they are just kicking it with Beeblax, just for whatevs. Beeblax is a cool bro, if a little needy, and also the easiest way to travel across galaxies on the cheap, and she would not mind just chilling with it for a minute, especially if it meant not having to do the stuff she is supposed to be doing—her job or whatever.

She wonders if the other hers are as feelingsy about the whole thing as she is, or if her emotionality is unique, the defining characteristic of herself and thus her universe. And then she thinks of Zarzak, watches it dancing in her mind, feels a warmth in her chest, sighs.

She is unable to get the Zarzak thought out of her mind, and finds herself unable to discern the goodness or badness of the thought. She can only experience it, watch the image in her mind's eye and feel the sensations rippling inside her. And even though she knows it is some space bullshit, it is pleasant.

"Oh Beeblax. 'Tell me, where is fancy bred? Or in the heart or in the head?'"

"I get that reference. I get all references. My knowledge of references is absolute. But there exist none who can swim in the reference pool of Beeblax. So like, what's the point of anything?"

"I kind of wanted to talk about my thing, but whatever, I guess. Just chill. You're dope as hell, Beeblax. I'm sure you'll find someone you can glop with."

"That's not what glop means, even in transconception."

"Okay, Beeblax. Okay."

"I'm kind of just dealing with some stuff right now and it's messing me up in ways beyond your reckoning."

"It's okay. I get it. It's cool."

The rest of the trip is quiet and kind of weird. At an appointed moment known only to Beeblax, it/they spits Aria out into the cosmos (without saying goodbye). She is submerged in impossible geometries and unthinkable colors as her mind struggles to readjust to her native umwelt. It's not that cool, though, so she doesn't really think about it. Soon enough, her particles begin to resonate at familiar frequencies, and the universe coheres, and she sees points of light whizzing past her, stars and planets and other space shit, as she flies through the darkness. A thin layer of Beeblax clings to her skin, which is mad gross but also it keeps her from dying.

She sees the cosmic being known as the Drowning King in the distance, arms flailing, body shaking, desperately clawing at the vast emptiness of eternity. No one knows how long the Drowning King has been drowning. He's maybe existed since forever, unable to breathe, unable to die—or perhaps dying very, very, very slowly.

As she comes closer, his figure grows larger and larger until her field of vision is completely filled with him. The jelly begins to burn as she enters his atmosphere, and, wreathed in golden jelly flames, she pretends that she is a phoenix. She lands on a crystal at the center of his crown, a diamond as expansive as an ocean. The jelly absorbs the impact of her landing, then sloughs off, and she notices a bulge in her pocket that was not there before.

She finds a personal cassette player and cassette tape wrapped in a note:

I'm not supposed to do stuff like this, but take it. It's the most perfect mixtape that could ever exist. Sorry for being a glop.

Sincerely, Beeblax

The label on the cassette tape says *Nothing Adds Up* in block letters.

The note bursts into sparks after she reads it, and Aria rolls her eyes before putting the tape and personal cassette player in her bag. She draws the Sister Ray—which is a cool space gun she stole from an uncool science bro who had mastered manipulation of matter but had not mastered avoiding punches to his face—and sets it to naviform mode, and fires on the ground beneath, intending to make use of some of that good good carbon. The material slowly rises up and begins to rearrange on an atomic level, slowly taking the shape of a vehicle. Aria uses the jetbike setting, as that is the dopest way of traveling across ancient, planet-sized alien gods, no doubt.

There are petals floating in the breeze, dozens of hundreds of them caught in the star-sweet exhalations of the Drowning King. Aria reaches out with her left hand to catch them as she flies, and then when she catches one, she gives herself a point; when she has twenty points, she turns up the speed of her jetbike a little more.

Already, she's accelerated past safety and reason, and she flies so fast now that the landscape is rendered into a blurry approximation of impressionist watercolors behind her. She can only just make out the petals before they are between her fingers, and it is increasingly difficult to distinguish reflex and intuition; this difficulty is pleasant to her, and she thinks that soon there will be no difficulty at all, only motion, and that she will lose herself in velvety self-abnegation, make herself into an animated koan. But when her hand is so full of petals that she can no longer snatch them from the air, she opens her palm and allows them all to drift away, and watches them flutter in the corner of her eye, feels the procession of silken tingles on her skin, pretends that the petals are emerging from inside. In these moments, she thinks that she might, in retrospect, forgive the universe for everything.

The Drowning King's eyebrow is a sort of strange forest, dense with lifeforms speciated somewhere in between plant and fungi clinging to massive hairs extending upwards past visibility. Aria's been riding for days now, and the scenery is a pleasant change from the vast, empty wastes of his starlit forehead. She could've taken a more direct route, but she has always been a romantic by nature, unable to resist the magic of the scenic route.

She thinks of Zarzak again and feels a delicious shiver, and then she tries very much not to think of Zarzak, which is extremely difficult—Zarzak is wonderful, wondrous, everything you could want and more. To not think of Zarzak is to not think at all. This is how the universe works now.

A cramp hits her stomach, and soon the pain is overwhelming. She pulls over next to a web of fuzz and blue-green slime protruding from one of the Drowning King's hairs and expels a throbbing lump of semi-solid pink from the hurt in her belly. The frequency of its vibrations begin to intensify, so as to harmonize with the neural oscillations of Aria's thoughts, and, having locked into a perfect fifth, the lump begins to expand, taking on a human figure, though still cast in pink stickiness.

"Agent Aria?" it buzzes. "This is Quark-4 transmitting from Star Station Emeraude. Do you read me?"

The pink cannot distinguish signal from noise, and the simulacrum continuously shakes, swirls, melts—Quark-4's features getting lost and found again in the tessellating flutters of afterimage and static. Was Quark angry? Worried? Sad? The voice betrayed nothing, and the face was chaos.

"Agent Aria," it says. "What is your status? Report immediately."

Aria runs her fingers along its shifting edges, tracing Quark as she remembers her, her lines, her angles, her smile. Aria had been real tight with Quark-3, who was super chill and great at kissing or whatever, but Quark-4 is an asshole, super serious and unsympathetic and kind of weird on social stuff.

"I'm here," says Aria. "Everything's cool. Just Aria, please."

"Status report."

"I'm on my way. Maybe a couple more days to the eye."

"Seventy percent of known galaxies have succumbed to the Zarzak Contagion. Within days, it will have expanded to the edge of the universe. All other agents have been lost. You are our only hope."

"Yeah, that's cool, but to be super clear here, I am not an agent. 'Slave' seems like a really harsh word, and I don't really want to use it because of some historical stuff on my home planet and my whole ethno-racial deal that you probably don't know about, but you have to really chill on the 'agent' talk."

"Agent Aria! You have one week to save the universe!"

Quark freezes on the last word. Her image is still deformed by time and distance, but the face is stuck in a pleading expression, mouth open, wide eyes, eyebrows arched along a sentimental curvature. Aria puts her finger in the nose. It's not super hilarious, but it is sort of funny.

The image deflates into a little pink ball, and Aria stores it back in her tummy hole before setting off again. As she rides, she thinks about how Zarzak has almost certainly spread to Earth, which means that everyone she has ever known has been affected.

It's funny to imagine the people she knew in her old life in love with a weird space monster. Derrick, who broke up with her for being "like, weirdly volatile about dumb stuff" is now in love with a space monster. Her ex-roommates Angie and Diane, who used to order pizza without telling her and secretly eat the pizza in Angie's room without telling Aria or asking if she wanted in, are now in love with a space monster. Funny, right? But then she thinks about her mom and her sisters and her middle school history teacher Mr. Jacobs and all the people she knew who were kind and of good will, and she feels sad for them, but also kind of happy for them too, because Zarzak is actually pretty amazing.

Aria decides to take a cigarette break at the edge of the Drowning King's eye, stopping next to a colossal metal structure which she hypothesizes is keeping the eyelid open. Balancing the Sister Ray in the crook of her right arm and leaning against her jetbike, Aria rolls a paper and some purple flakes into a cigarette. She puts it in her mouth and lights it with the tip of the Sister Ray. Space cigarettes are nicotineless garbage, but they're better than nothing. She closes her eyes and takes a long drag and holds it as long as she can, and her lungs hurt pleasantly, like they have been out in the summer sun too long.

She puts on the headphones and plays Beeblax's mixtape. It is mostly alien music, arrhythmic and atonal and difficult to listen to, and the cassette quality is not great. She gives it a chance for a few songs, but it is too terrible for her to bear, and she turns it off before the fourth song can begin. Her eyes are full of smoke when she opens them, and when it clears, she notices there is a braincube lurking across the way, on the edge of a canyonesque pore.

"Fuck," she says.

The braincube is eight feet by eight feet by eight feet of wrinkly, pink meat. It slides along the ground slowly, greasily, with a sound like an inverted burp. Aria rushes to her feet, but it is too late. Already, she can feel the braincube's poisonous thought-waves in her mind. Nausea. Pain. Ennui. Weltschmerz. Anomie. Heartbreak.

Loneliness.

All at once.

"Aria points the Sister Ray at the brain-cube," she says, "but then she realizes that she is saying that she is pointing the Sister Ray at the braincube rather than actually doing it. This is probably an effect of the toxic psychoradiation she is being bom-barded with."

Fuck you, braincube.

"It shambles ever closer, so close now that Aria's nostrils burn with the stink of sparked neurons and putrid glial resid-ues. Aria tries to once again distinguish between saying things and doing things, but it is difficult. She thinks this might be interesting from a philosophical perspec-tive, but she is probably going to die too quickly to really get into it."

The braincube is the worst of all pos-sible cubes.

"Drops of fear-sweat collect on her fore-head and glisten in the starlight. She strug-gles to move her feet. They do not move. She is desperate. She has to do something if she is not to be braincubed. She tries to think with the part of her brain that is not a brain but is actually a robot. She thinks she might—"

—be getting the hang of it again, but she is—

"—not sure if she has it yet. Or if she ever had it at all."

The anomie is not helping.

"Then, at the last possible moment—,"

Aria leaps back. The braincube is still up in her business, but there is room now for reprisal. She crouches and points the Sister Ray. She goes down, down-right, right, punch. This would cause her to shoot her raygun if this were a video game, but this is not a video game. It is real life. Again, toxic psychoradiation is some bullshit.

"Goddamn it," she says, before adding, "there is no God. We are all nothing in a sea of nothing."

The emotional pain is unbearable. Aria can barely remain conscious.

Baring its teeth, the bearcube rotates such that its mighty clawed corner comes down on Aria's face, adding physical pain to the mix. Blood pours from the wound, spraying Aria's shirt and the nearest side of the bearcube. The bearcube does not stop. It is relentless and without mercy. It spins around and around, murderously, and when it has cut her enough, it rolls itself on top of her body. She reaches out with her left hand to push it away, and the pain she experiences is as if she's plunged her hand directly into a star. Teeth tear and shred and gnash at her fingers. She tries to pull her hand away, but she is weak from pain and blood loss and also the bearcube is a real motherfucker. She cannot escape. She cannot breathe. This is it. This is the end. She can only look into the wall of fur and listen to the crackle of bones and—

Wait.

There isn't supposed to be blood inside of her. The fluids inside of her are purple and viscous and cold. Nor does she need to breathe. Like, it's a cool thing to do when you want to smell stuff, but it's not necessary for her survival. Plus, wasn't it a brain or something a minute ago? Nothing about this is adding up.

Wait.

Her fingers struggle to find the walkman at her waist. They will not remain steady. They tremble like she is telling a scary story or doing a magic trick. But soon they find their quarry. She presses play.

Almost. The bearcube shifts just as her index finger is on the button, pinning her hand down under its weight. The bearcube is everywhere and everything, and the world is going dark. She thinks she may be slipping in and out of consciousness, but it is difficult to tell. Was she unconscious just now? Or did she just blink? Does it matter? She cannot see anything anymore. It is not darkness. Darkness is a thing. She sees nothing. The void. The end.

"Fuck everything," she whispers.

She can't die here.

She summons all her remaining Aria- ness and tries to pull her hand from under the bearcube. It does not move. Too much weight on it. Then, redoubling her Aria- ness, and trying her very best to scream, she tries to wrench her other hand free of the bearcube's clutches. The intact pieces of meat and bone are stuck in the bear- cube's teeth, and it does not want to let go. It bites down harder. Aria pulls. This is not a pleasant experience.

When she's finished, she reaches over with the stump and slams it against the buttons on the walkman. Again and again. And then, there is music. An Earth song. Disco. A girl singing a song about lust over trippy synthesizers and trembling static.

The braincube is across the way, and Aria is not dying or dead. Awesome. The Sister Ray is still pointed at it. The music blasts in her ears, and she can no longer feel the braincube in her mind. She's about to pull the trigger, but she sees that the braincube is shaking slightly. She doesn't know if this is a natural part of the brain- cube's biology, or if the braincube is expe- riencing fear.

She lowers her raygun slightly. "What's your deal?" she asks.

There is a long wait, and then Aria ima- gines Zarzak and the braincube dancing together. The thought is gentle, fleeting, and at first she thinks it is just a stray imag- ining. But then, there is another image of Zarzak and the brain together, and then another. And Aria sees the braincube in her mind's eye, smaller now, alone amon- gst an array of bizarre xenostructures—a park maybe, a playground? And Aria sees the braincube alone, covered in a purple slime, surrounded by other braincubes in groups of three to five, also covered in slime. She sees a ship, hears an explosion, feels the sickly squeeze of hyperspace in her gut, all punctuated by images of Zarzak.

But then disaster.

The ship crashes, and the braincube is alone again, its brainbody bloodied, its transport reduced to rubble. In the end, the image of Zarzak is flashed over and over again. Zarzak. Zarzak. Zarzak. Zarzak. Zarzak. Zarzak. Zarzak.

"Okay. I get it."

The image fades.

Aria stomps her cigarette out and gets on her jetbike.

"Later," she says.

Before she can go, she is bombarded by images of the braincube dying, starving, murdered, dead. *A stack of braincubes teetering mournfully on braincube planet. The sound of silence.*

Aria looks back at the trembling cube. "What do you want?"

Zarzak. Zarzak. Zarzak. Zarzak. Zarzak. Zarzak. Zarzak.

"Stop doing that."

A small, simple ship, flying up and away from the Drowning King, escaping home-ward. Aria sighs.

"Fuck you," she says, but she straps the braincube to the back of the jetbike. It is very awkward. She does not like the squishy feeling of the braincube pushing on her back, and its size and shape completely mess up her aerodynamics and balance.

"We're not friends," she says, and they begin the journey across the eye.

Aria starts noticing them just after passing from sclera to iris. First, a single Driffle lying on the surface of the eye, bleeding cloudstuff from a wound at its side. Unable to speak its language, she seals its wound with the Sister Ray and goes about her business. Then there is a bruised Ceterian limping toward the pupil. Aria approaches to offer aid, but the Ceterian yells at her with all its mouths and is way uncool, so she bounces.

She sees more and more lifeforms as she travels, some of familiar species, some entirely new to her, each one traveling alone. Many are injured, but all those that are conscious persevere.

This is unexpected. To the extent that there exists mutually understood, enforce-able law across galaxies, visiting the Dro-wning King is a super-serious offense, as it is generally agreed across culture and species that fucking around with ancient space gods is not a good idea. Nobody wants to awaken anything that's gonna take over/destroy everything. Better to just leave shit alone. Aria had expected to see a few desperate types hanging out, possibly sent by their own planets to deal with this shit, but she had not anticipated seeing this surfeit of weirdos.

The brawl starts around the pupil, just as the Spire of Zarzak comes into view.

"Holy fuck," Aria says.

It extends for miles, and there are far too many participants to count. Millions at least. Aliens of all kinds, wondrous creatures with strange physiology and technology unknown on Aria's side of the universe, and all of them are going fucking ham. They punch each other with fists as large as boulders, choke each other with dripping tentacles, fly into the air and fire mind lasers, pilot shiny death robots and mechanized animal hybrids, sing songs that melt bones, etc. The fighting appears indiscriminate. There are no sides, no rules: just violence. There are screams of all sorts: pain, anger, fear—but Aria is capable of making out only one word:

"Zarzak."

These are the Fuckboys of Zarzak, the obsessives, the stalkers, the jealous assholes. Most lifeforms are content to keep Zarzak in their heart, quietly nursing a sweet, peaceful love that is patient and kind and crosses time and space without envy or anger. But these motherfuckers are clearly not keeping it together, and Aria is unsure how to proceed. She sees herself blasting the shit out of all of them with the Sister Ray, and for a moment, she is unsure if it is her own thought or the braincube's.

"I told you to stop doing that. It's not cool. Anyway, we need the power of chill vibes, not aggro shit," says Aria. But she allows herself to imagine blasting the shit out of all of them with the Sister Ray. It is a pleasant thought, especially with the knowledge that these people are all jerks perverting all that is beautiful and awesome about Zarzak, and she hopes that the braincube did not hear her think that. She puts Beeblax's mixtape on again, hoping there might be a song with the power of chill vibes on it. But no. Just more alien noise.

"I guess we do this the hard way."

Aria revs the jetbike and drives straight into the crowd, weaving through the combatants, dodging their attempts on her and each other. The ungainliness of the braincube is initially a hindrance, bringing her within a hair's breadth of getting decapitated by a giant psycho mantis and then burned by a living explosion and then brought asymptotically close to absolute zero by a slug guy.

But soon enough she settles into a rhythm, and she realizes that the fighting is not quite as indiscriminate as she first thought. There are some conventions, some strategy. The Fuckboys are trying to approach the Spire while also trying to keep all other fuckboys away from the Spire. Given the choice, most will focus their efforts more on preventing those behind them from progressing than impeding those already ahead of them. They all seem very angry that Aria is effectively cutting the line, but none of them do anything to stop her once she has passed.

It takes about a day to get through it all.

The base of the spire is a great machine drilling into the eye of the Drowning King. There are many Fuckboys here, and these ones seem extra rowdy, but there is also a golden robot calmly sitting on a long series of steps leading to the entrance, not fighting anyone. This is a surprise to Aria, as she had begun to forget that it was even possible to not be engaged in 24/7 fisti-cuffs. The Fuckboys mostly ignore the robot and the area immediately surrounding it. None follow Aria when she approaches it.

"Madness," says the robot when it sees her. "They have forgotten why they even started this journey in the first place."

"You speak English," says Aria.

"I am familiar with all the languages of this arm of the universe, and my subrou-tines generate probable languages at a rate of one million per cycle. You are a human of Earth, yes?"

"Basically. I'm from there, anyway."

"Yes. This truly is madness. All wish to enter this spire, yet none will deign to allow another entry. Their minds are clouded with a foolish passion."

"Yeah. That's kind of why I'm here."

The robot stands. "I am T.A.R.C.T.I.L., the Tactical Assault Robot Created to Incr-ease Love. I was designed to ensure the continued existence of love in this universe, yet I will never love or be loved myself."

"Oh. Cool. My name is Aria. It's not my real name, but I just sort of go by that now."

"Acceptable."

"So, uh, are you with Zarzak, or are you just chilling or what?"

"I have no formal affiliation with the being known as Zarzak, and I lack the capacity to experience the love of Zarzak as other sentients do. I am here of my own accord, to guard the gates of this spire and stop those who might interfere with Zarzak."

"And why is that?"

"I exist only for the propagation of love, and Zarzak is the fulfillment of love."

"What? No, that doesn't make any sense. That's dumb."

"All the universe now knows love. This is the fulfillment of love, the ultimate form of love, a love that enmeshes all."

"I mean, Zarzak's cool and all, but that's not what love is. Being forced to love a weird space monster is not love."

"Zarzak forces nothing. Zarzak asks nothing of those who love it. Zarzak plants the seed and allows it to flower. Does one ever choose to love? Love is always an imposition by fate and biology."

"It's still not real."

"What makes love real? If there is no difference between the thing and its simu-lacrum, then both are as real as the other."

"It's creepy and wrong. It's in my head, in everybody's head."

"Zarzak provides only warm feelings toward an abstraction. All may exist as they are, only with love in their hearts."

Uninterested in pursuing this line of inquiry further, Aria sighs and reaches for the Sister Ray. Before she can even touch it, T.A.R.C.T.I.L. grasps her wrist. Its grip is painful and unyielding. With its other hand, it holds a glowing laser pistol to her head.

"I do not wish to harm you, Aria, but I will do what I must. I am armed with the most advanced weaponry in the universe. I am trained in every martial practice. None can stand against T.A.R.C.T.I.L. when love is on the line."

Aria slowly raises her arms. "It's cool. I'm chill. I get it."

T.A.R.C.T.I.L. lets her go but keeps its weapon trained on her.

"If you wish to continue our discourse, I would allow it. If not, I will ask you to leave this place."

Aria nods, sits down, and begins talking. She tries to convince T.A.R.C.T.I.L. that it's wrong. The task is next to impossible. Aria martials every ounce of rhetorical ability within her, but is essentially only able to restate her core premises, i.e. that love of Zarzak is a violation of consent and that love created through artifice is both qualitatively distinct from and materially inferior to that love which might be called natural. Each of her arguments is met with a dozen counter-arguments, every premise is found contradictory, every conclusion is found wanting. T.A.R.C.T.I.L. weaves a web of rhetorical bullshit the likes of which Aria has never witnessed before. All the classical methods fail: Socratic, Hegelian, getting angry and saying a bunch of swears. There is no dialectic, no synthesis.

We are at Sophistry Level Infinity.

The braincube manages to tumble off the jetbike and squish over. Its awkward interjections of imagery and thought do little to progress the discourse, but Aria is able to find some comfort leaning against it as the hours and then days go by. Three whole days, at first filled with conversation, then mostly silent, as Aria can only occasionally summon a useful thought or concept. She goes so far as to engage T.A.R.C.T.I.L. on the nature of robotic epistemology and cyber-existentialism, attempting to leverage her own status as a cyborg to get into the nature of free will and emotion and materialism. She even throws in a few logical paradoxes.

No dice. T.A.R.C.T.I.L. is unmoved.

Aria and the braincube start playing a mental game on the second day, something from the cube's home planet. It is kind of like backgammon, but obscenely complex, and part of the game is thinking about the move you are going to make, which is different than thinking to make the move. After a full day of getting trounced, she feels that she is very close to winning, which doesn't matter because this game is dumb, but then she loses again, and she imagines herself flipping over the board in anger. And she realizes she is now truly into this game for real, as the pleasure of winning is dwarfed by the pain of defeat, and this sparks an epiphany.

"Hey robot."

"I am T.A.R.C.T.I.L."

"Yeah. I know. I was just thinking, isn't the very fact that I don't believe this love is real a sign that this love is unfulfilled and imperfect?"

"It is common for sentients to not understand that the emotions they experience are love."

"Yeah. Super common. Still imperfect. If your goal is the fulfillment of love, then shouldn't the universal knowledge of it be its ultimate form?"

"Perhaps."

"And you know, I think there's only one way peeps know for sure that the love they had was definitely, definitely real."

"And that is?"

"Take it away. Maybe you're in love, maybe you're not. It's hard to say in the moment. But then when it's gone, you can really feel it. Like somebody cut off an arm. Like somebody cut out your soul. Like somebody cut out your brain and put it in a space robot body. If you're right and the love is real, if I go in there and stop it, everyone will know what's up, that they experienced the truest, realest love possible. How is that not perfect?"

"Calculating. Please stand by."

T.A.R.C.T.I.L. just stands there for a while, frozen, and Aria is just like, whatever. She thought it was kind of a dumb argument, but it's cool that it worked. She tells the braincube to wait here. She gets the Zarzak. Zarzak. Zarzak. Zarzak. Zarzak. Zarzak. Zarzak from it again, but she is firm.

She tells the braincube to stay safe and make good decisions, and she gives it a little hug despite herself. She waves her hand in front of T.A.R.C.T.I.L.'s eyes a few times to be sure, and then she enters the Spire.

Zarzak is on a rotating pillar in the center of a small, red room at the top of the tower. The pillar throbs with strange, humming energy, presumably plumbed from within the Drowning King. Zarzak dances, fluid and shapeless, smoothly mimicking shapes as it flows across the pillar.

Aria has the Sister Ray pointed at Zarzak, but she cannot pull the trigger. Not because she loves Zarzak—no, definitely not that—but because she feels that there should be more to it than this, more than just another moment. She has been dicking around on this mission for like two weeks, and she deserves a little drama, a little acknowledgement. She wants to be witnessed.

She fires a warning shot and waves.

"Hey! Hello. Over here! I am Aria! I am from a planet called Earth. We have lots of cool things there. Like, uh, cats. And phones that have games on them. Chess. Democracy. Samosas. The French New Wave. Pirates. TV on the Radio. And TVs and radios. I mean, I haven't been back in a while. It's complicated. I'm not really 'human' or whatever anymore. I'm still trying to work out a good portmanteau. Starborg? Robogal? Something like that, but

     INFINITE LOVE ENGINE

not dumb. Anyway, I am here on behalf of the Star Syndicate to fuck you up."

Zarzak says nothing, but shapes itself into an abstract humanoid form, a ball floating above fleshy curves, and it dances.

Aria comes closer. "Who are you? Why are you doing this?"

Zarzak dances. Aria tries to read the movements, tries to see an unctuous smirk and a cackle and a speech about being the most desired being in the universe or a pathetic snivel about wanting to be loved or a noble yet misguided diatribe on the mind-killing evils of loneliness. Something.

Anything.

But no.

Zarzak just dances.

Beautifully.

Aria does not know who built this place, if it was Zarzak or someone else, if Zarzak is conqueror or prisoner, monster or victim. She comes closer and closer.

It is said that the Sister Ray can kill gods. It is ancient and unknowable, like everything that matters. She points it at Zarzak, and Zarzak dances.

"This sucks," she says.

She is going to pull the trigger. Totally. In just a second. Just a second. It is just very pleasant being here right now. Aria feels clean inside, not happy exactly, but clean, or maybe healed, and it is a nice sensation, again pleasant. Why not linger a while? It's not like there's exactly a time limit. Well, Quark said there was a time limit, but Quark is a doofus. No one ever got hurt by just hanging out. Just for a minute.

Aria begins to dance.

It's fun.

She offers Zarzak the Sister Ray. It slides a protrusion toward her and takes the Sister Ray.

Aria keeps dancing. She thinks it was probably a mistake to do that just now, and she thinks that she probably should have just shot it. She has never been good at just shooting things. She is too sentimental, too much of a romantic, too inclined toward forgiveness and non-violent talky times. The Zarzak Contagion is definitely way stronger up close, and she wishes she had considered that in advance.

Zarzak points the weapon at Aria.

"Shit. So you're, like, definitely a bad guy, huh? Not even a cool bad guy. Just a dick."

Aria wants to think of a cool thought before she dies, but she can't really think of anything but how great Zarzak is.

Bummer.

But before she can be murdered, the doors of the Spire fly open and T.A.R.C.T.I.L. appears, covered in weapons—lasercannons and glowswords and particle whips extending from compartments all over its body. It charges them, and Aria is unsure which one it is after. Zarzak does not seem to care either way.

It fires wildly, dance-dodging an incoming volley of ultra-missiles and laser spray. Aria does not dodge but somehow manages to avoid getting hit. In the confusion, she leaps forward and reaches out for the Sister Ray. There is a quick tug of war, but Zarzak doesn't even have real muscles. She takes the weapon and aims.

"You suck, dude. Like really."

And she fires. Zarzak is hit directly, and Aria holds the beam down on it, causing Zarzak to be rearranged on a quantum level. It is totally dope.

She stands, dusts herself off. Already, she can feel her mind getting right. Emotions are dumb, she decides. As a way-cool space cyborg, she should know better than to be seduced by a few warm fuzzies. She looks over to T.A.R.C.T.I.L., ready to continue the fight if necessary. It lies on the ground, bleeding from its left side.

Wait.

She puts on her headphones again and presses play, and she sees the braincube there, missing many of its most important atoms. It didn't get a full blast, but even a taste of the Sister Ray is enough to fuck up one's shit.

Aria rushes over to the dying cube. And she is like, "Why?"

And the memory rushes in Aria's mind.

Aria sighs.

"*Fuck you,*" *she says, but she straps the braincube to the back of the jetbike. It is very awkward. She doesn't like the squishy feeling of the braincube pushing on her back, and its size and shape completely mess up her aerodynamics and balance.*

And the braincube shows her all the times it was alone on braincube planet again, and then it shows them traveling and hanging out and playing mind games, and then the braincube dies.

Zarzak's dance pillar begins to pulse, and the hum turns to a sickly screech. Without Zarzak doing whatever dumb thing he was doing, the equipment is freaking out. Or maybe the Drowning King just wants to get all of this stupid shit out of his eye. Either way, Aria has a feeling shit is about to get real.

She sighs.

"You're carbon-based, right?"

She sets the Sister Ray to naviform mode, and she forms the braincorpse into a little ship. Nothing special, just dece enough to get them out of atmo. She really wishes she knew what the braincube's actual name was, but she just names it the Braincube. It's sort of cute, she thinks.

She gets into Braincube and flies away just as the Spire explodes. The universe is saved. Hurray. Great job.

As the Drowning King shrinks in the distance, Aria wonders, idly, if souls can attach to atoms or if they are more of a molecular thing. She does not know the answer, but she likes the idea of it.

"Tell me, Braincube. Where is fancy bred? Or in the heart or in the head?"

INFINITE LOVE ENGINE

It is engendered in the eyes, she thinks, and she does not know if she is thinking it herself or if someone is thinking it for her or if she is just thinking about someone thinking it for her because she is a big softie. Is this a kind of love, this inability to distinguish sentiment from sentimentality? Perhaps T.A.R.C.T.I.L's premise was wrong. Perhaps love already exists in infinite quantities all around us, subtly connecting us all together with little moments of affection and kindness and not attached to freaky alien buttholes.

"Okay. We can be friends now," she says.

KANISHK TANTIA

A WOMB ACROSS TIME AND SPACE

Tasminah eyed the merchant.

Until today, the people had known her as someone of great import, of means and riches. Now, she was simply Tasminah, one of the many faceless immigrants seeking off-world passage in the wake of political tumult. And unless the Eleventh Moon found her and took her back to the royal family, she would remain Tasminah. It was an identity she forged for herself, but one that came with the baggage of a life.

She knew the merchant as only the merchant. He was a fixture of the city, his job and identity melded into one. He accepted this, even advertised himself as "the merchant." Not everyone had a need for a unique identity, or indeed the privilege of forging one for themselves.

"How much?" Tasminah kept her questions short and vague. The Port Authority claimed to have spies everywhere.

"Six years."

"Three."

"Six."

"Four?" Tasminah knew she had erred as soon as the word left her mouth. Still, she attempted to correct herself. "Four."

The merchant shook his head. "Six. The Temur does not negotiate, as you well know."

  A WOMB ACROSS TIME AND SPACE

"The Temur can—" She bit back a remark that would surely have bumped the price to seven. "Five is—"

"Six." The genial smile looked more fixed with each word. Out of the corner of her eye, Tasminah noticed two hulking automatons, bronzed bodies glinting in the stifling sun. Had they always been there?

"Six." She exhaled, and a bead of sweat trickled down her nape. "I can do six."

"Marvelous." The merchant puffed delightedly on a small silver pipe, and a wisp of orange smoke rose and joined the stains its brethren had made on the ceiling. "Stable 7-A. Ask for Makal. He'll arrange the implantation."

Tasminah stalked out onto the bustling street, running the numbers in her head. Six years inside a Temur was a long time, but she could handle it. She would have to.

The smell of rotting hay and damp wood permeated the air of Stable 7-A. Tasminah's feet stuck to the floor, coming away with a soft squelch as she practically fought her way towards the Temur she would call home for the next six years.

The beast stood nearly four times the height of a large man. Its seven legs—pillars of scarred, lumpy flesh—carried the pulsating, copper-furred mass that hosted its womb. A putrid, cloying stench rolled off the Temur's body, the sickening odor of dirt and fluids best left unnamed. Every so often, an eye popped open, stared listlessly, and then moved underneath the fur to a new location, where it repeated the action. A graceless creature.

Tasminah breathed a sigh of relief. The merchant had not lied.

Six years within the womb of the grotesque animal before her. It would be a long journey, but the Port Authorities would not find her, would not even know of her existence. It was the Temur's great gift, the boon that creation had bestowed upon it as a meager apology for its accursed form.

Tricking the fabric of reality and escaping into hiding beyond the cosmos must have been taxing; the Temur had little intellectual capacity. Upon feeling a living organism within its womb, the Temur had assumed it was pregnant and let instinct take over.

Tasminah's eyes dampened as she rubbed the creature's wiry fur. Temurs had been mythical beasts once, steeped in legend and mystique. But the sad, tortured thing before her had no such airs about it. Makal himself was behind a screen, controlling robotic arms that had already finished opening the Temur.

Two gore-spattered half-moons with blood-matted hair stretched away from the Temur's body, providing a pathway for her to enter. The beast brayed in pain, a cacophonous sound that shook within Tasminah's ears. It could not melt into the ether yet, not while its belly lay sliced open. The robotic arms, dripping with the Temur's crimson-black blood, waited for Tasminah to enter her new home.

KANISHK TANTIA

A few months—a year even—she could have done. But the Temur before her had a gestation period of six years. Six years of battle to retain her identity and sense of self, but Tasminah's only alternative was death at the hands of the Eleventh Moon. If all went according to plan, she would be reborn on a new world, a distant memory for those who hunted her.

Tasminah did not make a fuss as the beast roared in her face, droplets of yellow mucus splattering over her body. She did not gag as she gingerly stepped into the sodden, pulsing innards of her new home. She barely even fidgeted as the glistening flesh closed around her and the walls of the Temur's body trapped her in a warm, wet embrace. The pathway to the outside world sealed shut, and she settled into a moist darkness.

Biological stasis took over her body as the Temur, mistaking her for a gestating fetus, prepared to flee the clutches of time. Tasminah's hair and nails ceased to lengthen, her blood ceased to flow, and yet, her body continued to function. Already she could feel her mind floating away, her sense of identity under assault by the Temur. Unhitched from her body, her mind would slowly erode as she forgot her story, her likes and dislikes, and eventually, even her name.

She heard her father's voice:

Find your cornerstone, Minah. The anchor of your identity.

Her old anchor had been the day that her father had named her Eleventh Moon. Before that, her birthdays, her family, her mother. This time, Tasminah pictured her brother as he played with a pearl-handled dagger, twirling it between his fingers as the family ate dinner.

The Temur's heartbeat pulsed, a low drumbeat in the background, a meditative reverberation that Tasminah could feel in her bones. Its blood rushed all around her, the digestive processes of the creature a rushing din.

And amidst that din, she heard something unexpected.

A rustle, a squelch, and movement.

Implanted in the womb of the Timur, Tasminah wasn't alone.

Dargah's identity was of his own making, but not his own design. He forged it through blood and steel, through whispered conversations in the dark and surreptitious exchanges of money. He was the man who sat in an unlit corner of the bar, nursing a single drink, while the innkeeper shot glances at him and pretended to wipe glasses. Dargah, an identity accompanied by the gentle schlick of a blade sliding between the ribs.

Dargah shot out an arm to cover the girl's mouth, accurately estimating where it would be even in the total darkness of the womb.

"Silence. Or we shall frighten the beast."

Rather than comply with the request, Tasminah bit into Dargah's hand, drawing blood. It was by an effort of will and training that Dargah did not himself succumb to hypocrisy by screaming at the pain. He did, however, promptly withdraw his hand.

"Wh—Who are you?"

"Inconsequential." Dargah kept his voice low. Speaking was a luxury that he rarely entertained.

"Why are you—"

Dargah did not care for the girl's questions. Instead, he stated the only relevant fact that he knew.

"One of us needs to die."

"I'm sorry, what?"

"The merchant has clearly oversold his Temur," Dargah repeated. "So, either one of us dies, or we both do."

Dargah wondered if speaking out loud had been a mistake. Perhaps he ought to have killed her already, but even an assassin has principles. He did not like killing those unprepared for death, or killing without cause.

"I—" There was uncertainty in the girl's voice. "Let's start over. I'm Tasminah."

"Tasminah, one of us needs to die. And it will not be me."

"A name, if you please."

"Dargah." He gave his name with pride. It was a calling card for those who knew.

"Well, Dargah, I don't see why one of us needs to—"

"Think." Dargah controlled his breathing, preparing to strike. "The Temur will soon realize our presence and hide itself."

"I know the mechanics of the—"

"When it does, our minds will tear away. They will spread across the cosmos, as our neurons struggle to remain connected across a sea of stars."

"I've trained at the Palace," Tasminah's voice was urgent, pleading. "I've spent plenty of time within Temurs."

"It will not matter."

"It will. The Beast won't notice, it's dumb, far too—"

Tasminah was trying to keep him talking, but she was out of time. Unprepared or not, he would deal with her. Thick, well-practiced fingers reached out towards Tasminah, scrabbling for her throat. It would only take seconds.

He felt the familiar wrenching sensation as the Temur pulled his mind out of his skull. His thoughts grew fuzzy, and a gray film descended over his eyes. His body fell away, the physical processes caught in stasis, while his mind broke from its cage of flesh and bone that held it and bled into the cosmos.

Fuck.

Like all Moon Children, Tasminah trained for years to withstand the Temur's effects on her mind. A bed, food, water. Unnecessary for the body, which would remain in stasis within the Temur, but such

 A WOMB ACROSS TIME AND SPACE

frivolities of the mind would help her maintain normalcy and, she hoped, sanity.

A room materialized around her—midnight blue walls, studded with silver dots that sparkled like distant stars. She stretched out on creamy white sheets, luxuriating in the feeling of silk against her skin. Her books lined the stained oak shelves, tomes of history, politics, language, and biology, memorized long ago. In the corner, a jug of water that never ran out and a bottomless chest of sweets and delicacies. Nourishment for the body, soul, and mind.

Tasminah knew her bedroom well. And her bedroom did not have a man in it.

And yet, a man wearing black robes stood impetuously in his shoes, running his fingers across his shaved head.

Dargah whistled as his eyes took in his surroundings. "Well, this is nice, certainly."

"Get out."

"Gladly." Dargah gave a mocking half-bow. "And where's the door, your highness?"

Tasminah gestured at an empty spot on the wall and frowned, realization dawning on her. No doors, no windows. There was nowhere else to go within the construct, and therefore no way to get there.

As the confusion and the anger settled within her, Tasminah felt the room shift away. The walls dissolved, the jug, the chest, the sheets—everything simply vanished. Instead, blood-stained sand covered the floor. Dargah had abandoned his robes and was shirtless, lying on a mat. His body shone

with the sweat of exertion, and his muscles flexed as he twisted his body.

Tasminah grimaced. Military. She should have guessed.

"Your shelter, I presume?"

Dargah smiled, snapping to his feet with military precision. "Precisely. Less comfortable, more utilitarian. Nothing passes the time like exercise."

Tasminah shook her head, hoping the movement would clear her thoughts. She pictured her room, her cornerstone, and briefly reasserted control. The sand sifted through the floor, midnight blue walls closed in around them, and silken sheets swaddled her once more. She shot Dargah a defiant smirk.

Dargah's face twisted in frustration, and soon the floor tiles were dissolving into coarse sand. The citrusy incense of her room turned to sour, sweat-soaked air, and they were back in the arena.

Wordlessly, they switched back and forth, over and over, until they both collapsed, panting.

"We can't—"

"No." Tasminah agreed. "We can't." "The arena—"

"Is no place for a lady to sleep."

"...will prevent us from going insane." Dargah's eyes narrowed. "If I could kill you—"

"But you can't." Tasminah grinned and wiped a hand across her brow. "And if we do nothing but train, sleep on sand

and eat dried meat and bread, we'll go insane all the same."

They sat in silence as the shelter switched back and forth between the arena and the bedroom.

Tasminah broke the silence. "Truce?"

For the first two years, Dargah spent every day wishing that he killed Tasminah before the Temur had hidden them away. They alternated between Tasminah's bedroom and Dargah's arena. At the arena, Tasminah would watch and jeer and tell Dargah that her father, the Tenth Moon, had possessed superior technique.

In the meantime, he could feel the cosmos ravage his sense of self. The illusion of the arena and the bed helped, but he was forgetting certain things. The taste of mead was no longer on his tongue. He had no family to recall, but he had sworn to remember those who had fallen at his hands. It was worrying that the earliest of those faces were blurring away.

Two years after their journey began, Tasminah approached him.

"Teach me."

"No," he grunted as he continued to spin in the sand, counterbalancing the spear he had chosen for the day's training with his own bodyweight. "Go away."

"Why?"

Dargah dodged an imagined fist and disemboweled an imagined opponent.

"Perhaps if I forget the mechanics of speech, you'd leave me alone."

Tasminah smiled. "Probably not. Why not train me?"

"Because there's nothing in it for me."

Tasminah watched as he rolled on the ground. "Yes, there is." She stalked over to the rack of weapons and picked out a wooden sword. "There definitely is."

"And what, pray, may that be?"

With a smile, she hefted the sword.

"You'll get to fight me."

Four years into the journey, Tasminah knew she was better off than she would've been alone, languishing in her bedroom.

Dargah remained a mystery. Training together hadn't made him less aloof. Every night, he slept on the floor, even though Tasminah offered to switch places with him. He spoke little, and when he did, it was mainly to correct her form.

And while the training was keeping her from going insane, it provided little fortification for her mind. The face of her father had blurred. Her mother was a warm memory in the distance. The only people she could clearly visualize were Dargah and her brother.

She was sure Dargah felt it too.

"I need your help." Dargah flipped around to face her from the floor as she reclined on the creamy silken sheets of her bed. "And I have something to offer you."

     A WOMB ACROSS TIME AND SPACE

Tasminah raised her brows and glanced at him over the top of her book. She couldn't resist throwing the words back in his face, although she did so teasingly.

"And what, pray, may that be?"

"A mutually beneficial deal." Dargah paused, and Tasminah could have sworn he almost cracked a smile. "We should recount stories to each other. As many as we can. About ourselves."

"Why?"

"Because I'm forgetting myself." Dargah was clearly unaccustomed to asking for aid, and Tasminah could sense his discomfort. "This way, we'll both remember."

"If not our own stories, then each other's."

"Exactly."

Nearly six years passed.

Dargah and Tasminah's minds had spread out, their neurons entangled but still separable. With careful thought, the two could recreate their distinct personalities, could remember themselves.

Dargah was quietly grateful that he had not killed Tasminah in the belly of the Temur. Her companionship fortified his mind. Sharing their stories brought them closer, creating an intimate knowledge between them.

Tasminah's stories revolved around her father and grandfather and brother. She talked of them, the Ninth, Tenth, and Eleventh Moons, high priests of their planet and her only family. She spoke fondly of her father, who named her Eleventh Moon on her tenth birthday. She spoke of the harsh training she underwent, the books she read, the dignitaries she met and despised.

Dargah's stories were shorter. He never elaborated, only speaking in simple terms of the deals he had made and the people he had killed. It brought him a grim satisfaction when Tasminah jumped at the tales or remarked that she had known some of his victims.

As they rested in Tasminah's bedroom, minds sore after yet another day of training, Tasminah looked at Dargah and asked the question that brought down the last wall between them.

"What's your cornerstone?"

Though he knew what the truth would bring, Dargah couldn't lie. Six years together, and each could tell when the other was lying.

"The Eleventh Moon."

"My brother?" Tasminah's eyes shot up, and Dargah saw the pathways of her brain light up as she processed the information.

"My last client."

"You killed—"

"The Tenth Moon."

"—my father."

There was a flicker of contrition in Dargah's eyes, but it vanished the moment Tasminah saw it.

Scaling the palace walls, waiting silently in shadows until the Tenth Moon retired for the night, killing him quickly and silently. It had been a difficult task, one any other assassin would build a legacy on. But professional pride gave way to unprofessional sorrow, for Dargah felt Tasminah's mind as closely as his own.

"That dagger with the pearl handle— that wasn't yours."

"No. Useless, ornamental thing." Dargah snorted, his brow wrinkling in a look of condescension. "I don't use antiques to kill. I stabbed him with it after he was already dead."

"Father gave one to each of us. Me and my brother." Tasminah turned around and stared at the ceiling, watching the specks of silver glimmer against the midnight blue. "Mine was missing on the day he was killed."

"I'm sorry," Dargah said. "Your brother is—"

"A bastard."

"A *dishonorable* bastard."

As Tasminah closed her eyes, tears streaking down her face, Dargah imagined the face of the Eleventh Moon. The man who approached him in a market with a pearl-handled dagger, promising safe passage and a hefty fortune on his word as a noble. He hadn't needed much convincing, but the betrayal had stung nonetheless.

Perhaps one day, Dargah would show the Eleventh Moon why assassins don't require written contracts.

Six years and a month.

Then two. Three. Twelve.

Slowly, as the days stretched on, horror set in.

Something had gone awry. Tasminah looked at Dargah, a creeping realization dawning on her face.

"Two people." A strangled whisper escaped her throat, "Twins."

"Twice the time." Dargah nodded. Sitting down on the coarse grains of sand, he began to stretch once more. "Twelve years."

Tasminah joined him and started running through the drills.

Twelve years.

Eight years together, and their identities began to bend and break, twisting into each other. They struggled now to remember who owned which story. As time wore on, the distinction became less important. The only things that mattered were survival and sanity, which they would only find together, not alone.

Tasminah knew now how to match every stroke Dargah made. He feinted, and she refused to fall for it. He struck. She parried. While they had once filled the arena with her yelps of pain, now the only sounds were the sharp ring of metal on metal and the two combatants' heavy breathing.

"Teach me to read."

Even after eight years together, with their brains slowly mirroring each other and every thought laid bare, Dargah did not often make requests. "Please?"

     A WOMB ACROSS TIME AND SPACE

"No." Tasminah grinned as she stared at the bright blue sky above. "Go away."

Dargah had never admitted it before, but she had suspected as much. He took payment upfront, in coins and cash, and signed nothing. He showed no interest in the books in her bedroom, although when she read out loud, he listened with rapt attention.

"There's something in it for you." Dargah's face broke into a smile.

"And what—"

"Pray—"

"May that be?"

They didn't need to say it out loud.

Whenever Dargah attempted to strike, Tasminah parried. She knew there was only one thing he would offer, and only one offer she would accept.

Reading, Dargah decided, was awful. For three months, he struggled with the oddly shaped runes until they felt familiar in his mind, but it took a year for Tasminah to call him "literate."

It helped that he could feel Tasminah's mind process letters and words and mimic the neural pathways that lit up as she read a passage. Alone, he may never have mastered the art at all. With Tasminah, his comprehension grew rapidly. She exposed him to the deepest recesses of her mind, and within those, he found the selections she had memorized. Philosophy. Art. Politics. Romance. Literature that he consumed as

though he were a parched man discovering an oasis of fresh water.

"These books are wrong." Dargah knew that Tasminah already suspected as much, for their minds were now indistinguishable. "Propaganda at best, lies at worst."

They had long ago stopped switching between arena and bedroom. Instead, their minds had stitched the two together, a vast bedroom with a single door that led to a sandy arena. Dargah stood at the threshold, holding a book on the History of the Moons, watching Tasminah lay waste to an army of imagined opponents.

Taminah paused her drills. "My father was a great man." Her voice invited argument. "He loved our planet and its people."

"No. He was a bastard, like his father, and your brother." Dargah sighed. "And you know it to be true."

"He restarted off-world trade—" Tasminah spoke half-heartedly. She knew the reply that was coming.

"So he could tax merchants into oblivion," he countered. "Why else would the merchant oversell the Temur? He was probably desperate."

Tasminah grabbed two swords from the rack and threw one at Dargah. He caught the handle, set the book down, and walked into the arena. As soon as he was ready, she charged at him, the glinting steel in her hands blazing towards his body.

"What about the dams?" Tasminah asked, her smooth movements almost flowing past his guard. "Cheap electricity for everyone."

"He exported most of it to other planets for profit. And millions died when the rivers dried up." Dargah's movements were more economical, and he beat the steel back with the handle of his blade. "He was disastrous."

"My brother is still a bastard for killing him." Tasminah sidestepped the jab Dargah had transitioned into.

"Yes, he is. But no less than your father."

There was no more repartee, and the air filled with the sound of clanging metal.

When the two retired, Dargah broached the subject once more. "So, will you become the Twelfth Moon still?"

For a few minutes, there was silence. Tasminah fixated on the sand, tracing patterns within it.

Finally, she spoke in a resigned tone. "I'll have to. My brother will come for me."

Despite their training, they had lost track of time and the Temur's tug came as a shock. In the past, they would have willingly re-entered their physical bodies, gathering as much of themselves from the vast cosmos as they could, some sense of identity hopefully intact.

But now? Dargah and Tasminah could not return to their individual selves, no more than bronze can separate back to copper and tin. When the Temur ejected them, it poured the mixture into the physical shells and returned them together.

Stable 7-A filled with the odious scent of sour amniotic fluid as the roaring beast ejected two gore-splattered bodies. Squawking and screaming, the Temur pushed first Tasminah, and then Dargah out, its muscular legs straining as it rid itself of the unwanted cargo.

Two bodies with one identity.

They looked at each other. Words were unimportant.

The merchant had not lied. Twelve years ago, the cargo ship had set out for a new world to deposit its contents. Six years ago, it completed the first leg of its journey and traveled back to the homeworld Tasminah and Dargah had once run from, where the Eleventh Moon reigned still.

A stunned guard looked at them before scrambling behind his counter. Tasminah prepared to leap towards the guard and snap his neck, but before she could do so, Dargah's hand landed on her shoulder. The guard was offering towels and blankets.

It only took a few hours for Dargah and Tasminah to ascertain that the Eleventh Moon did not want either of them.

"As I keep telling you, there is no Eleventh Moon. Not for a decade." The guard was frustrated. "You've been in there for a while, I know."

"There must be. The Moon family? I mean, you know who the Moon family is, right?"

"Lady, I'm not stupid." He sighed and repeated himself once more. "Nine years ago, the Eleventh Moon abdicated his position. Peaceful transition of power, yada yada. We're a democracy now."

For twelve years within the belly of the Temur, Tasminah and Dargah had prepared for this day. They had prepared for the Eleventh Moon to find them, arrest them, execute them. Now, they found him gone.

"Where is he now?" Dargah interrupted. "The Eleventh Moon?"

"Offworld, I think? Dunno."

Tasminah and Dargah could do nothing but stare at each other.

"Well, what do we—"

"Do now? We could always—"

"Hunt him down."

The guard seemed bemused by their behavior, but once they stopped, he cleared his throat. "Look, I don't know what you're up to. Murder is, of course, illegal. Sue him in a tribunal if you want. But until then—" He dug into a drawer and pulled out a thick paper booklet. "Welcome to the Democratic World of Az'Thurmond. Here's enough money to last each of you six months. There's an inn down the street that'll host you. Now, leave. I got other work to do."

Dargah and Tasminah nursed their food. Dried strips of jerky, two large tankards of blackberry mead, and a small bowl of sweets that Dargah had demolished twice over.

"We could just live in peace." Tasminah broke the comfortable silence they had settled into. "No need to fight if we don't have to."

For the first time in his waking life, Dargah read. The innkeeper helpfully provided a map of the area, and although Dargah recognized many of the streets, a lot had changed over twelve years. He jabbed a thick finger down.

"Bookstore?"

"Bookstore." Tasminah nodded, but then pointed elsewhere. "Blacksmith?"

"Blacksmith. Arena?"

"Definitely."

Two identities. Forged through birth and expectation, neither the princess nor the assassin alone could have broken the shackles that constrained their lives. But neither existed alone anymore. Tasminah and Dargah were more than friends, or lovers, or family. They were a single soul, forged within the womb of a beast unhitched from time.

A single soul at peace.

CASEY LANDERKIN is an artist/illustrator based in Philadelphia PA. She likes to make things, maybe even obsessed with making things, maybe she can't stop making things. Thankfully, she can put all the things she makes where you can find them online. She is interested in magic, fish, cooking, and a bunch of other stuff. This paragraph would be too long if she kept on listing the things that she finds interesting.

✩ ✩ ✩

Planet Scumm conducted this interview with Casey via email. Some text has been lightly edited for clarity.

ARTIST SPOTLIGHT

CASEY LANDERKIN

PLANET SCUMM: Tell us a little about your art background. What brought you towards painting such immersive and fantastical landscapes?

CASEY LANDERKIN: I went to Syracuse University where I received a BFA in Illustration, but I had been making art long before then. Most of the time making things was a compulsion, almost a tick. It became a way for me to concentrate, stay grounded and process life.

Just like many artists, the natural world is a huge inspiration to me. I like to combine the landscapes from my waking life with the landscapes of my dreaming life in my artwork because they are one in the same. I like showing people the world in that way.

You're so good at conveying ~*mood*~ even without a human subject. Is that tone something you choose to convey ahead of time, or does the vibe all come together as you're painting?

When making art, of any sort, there is always an oscillation between what you intended the piece to be and what the piece actually wants to be. I usually start with a hint of an idea and during the making process, I make compromises with the piece itself, which is how I feel I retain life inside the work. Sometimes pencil marks and brushstrokes cannot be corralled, and you have to just go along for the ride.

Let's talk about your process when you designed your *Planet Scumm* cover. How do you approach an adaptive project?

Is it more difficult to design these fantasy landscapes if you're matching a written description, rather than working from your imagination?

The idea for this piece came to me immediately, mostly thanks to the story itself. It was so well written and felt that I understood the way that the author described the landscape almost instantly. The idea didn't change much from the sketches to the final, it stayed the same because the story and my idea excited me so much.

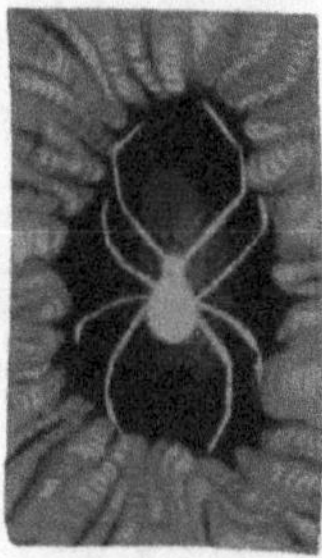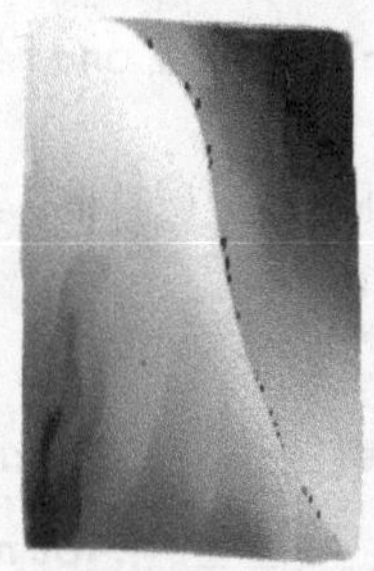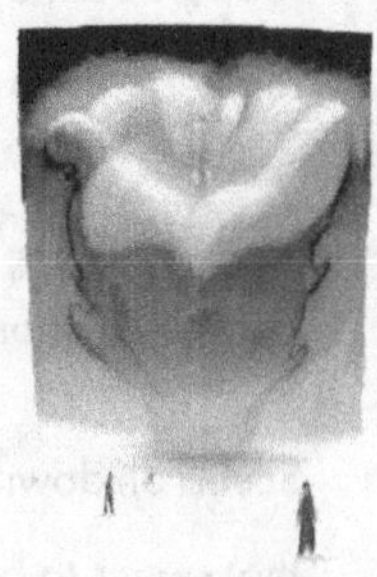

Thumbnails from early stages of development, inspired by the classic sci-fi art of Syd Mead and John Harris.

What is your favorite and/or your least favorite part of the creative process?

My favorite part of the creative process is the the initial moment of inspiration. It feels like your brain is a net and you are just catching ideas from the ether, which is always an exciting puzzle. The worst part is losing steam when a piece of work seems to slip away from you. Sometimes the need or want to make a work can just suddenly evaporate for no reason.

Who are the artists that most inspire you?

Some of my favorite artists are Hilma Af Klint, Carrie Mae Weems, Olafur Eliasson, Zarina Hashmi, Andrew Hem, and Sasha Gordon.

When you read fiction, do you crave more escapism or catharsis?

I think I enjoy both equally, I think these two things can be interchangable.

Do you have a favorite flavor, or sub-genre, of science fiction? What about it appeals to you?

My favorite type of sci-fi media are ones that dip into philosophical ideas. I prefer stories that almost feel like an allegory or a myth, ones that present questions about who we are, why we're here, and what will become of us. Some favorite movies are ones like *Contact*, *Annihilation*, and *Arrival*. Some favorite books are *Stories of Your Life* by Ted Chang, *Dawn* by Octavia Butler, and *Sphere* by Michael Crichton.

FIND MORE FROM CASEY LANDERKIN

» *on instagram at @caseylanderkin*   » *on tiktok at @clanderkin*   » *website at caseylanderkin.com*

SAVE THE OCEANS THE S.C.U.M.M. WAY

Today's Earthers treat their planet's bluer half with ______ disregard. Someone
[adjective]

really ought to come up with an acronymic solution, and FAST!

Chill out, ____breath. Someone already has! Just (___) these five, (______) steps
(animal)   *verb*   *adjective*

and you'll soon be in the (______).
adjective

Scuba on down there and (___) what needs (__________). Make note of anything
verb   *verb ending in ing*

that seems to be dying or encrusted in (___________). You may be down there
industrial byproduct

a while so consider packing some (_______).
plural snack

Cut throats. Time to find the (__________) responsible and (___) them up good.
plural derisive term   *verb*

You may be met with resistance, so consider packing some (_________).
plural weapon

Use nukes. Some things are beyond fixing! A few (___)bombs with (______)
insect   *greek letter*

reactors will dry things up lickety (__________).
gymnastic position

Mine rare metals. Once you've cleared away the organic matter with a

cleansing (________), (___) everything worth taking before the Earth (________
chemical reaction   *verb*   *governmental*

____________) can detain you.
body or military branch

Make a new planet. A better one! With (______) and (________) and days that
plural vice   *plural delicacy*

last for (______) and nights that make you feel (______) again. If you are in
length of time   *age, in years*

a hurry, consider (___)ing a pre-fab planet from a licensed broker.
verb

There! Easy! Now get your scuba gear and (___)!
verb

This Public Service Announcement begrudgingly brought to you by the nonprofit

(___) of Planet Scumm, (_______) for a Less (______) Tomorrow.
limb   *plural noun*   *Adjective*